A DANGEROUS
INHERITANCE

A DANGEROUS INHERITANCE

Patsy Smith

Published by Patricia Smith Publishing in conjunction with Writersworld, this book is produced entirely in the UK, is available to order from most book shops in the United Kingdom, and is globally available via UK-based Internet book retailers.

ISBN: 978-1-8380074-0-9

Cover Design by Jag Lall
Photo Credits:
Image by PublicDomainPictures from Pixabay
Free Stock Textures

Copy editor: Sue Croft

WRITERSWORLD
2 Bear Close, Woodstock,
Oxfordshire
OX20 1JX
United Kingdom

Tel 01993 312500

www.writersworld.co.uk

The text pages of this book are produced via an independent certification process that ensures the trees from which the paper is produced comes from well managed sources that exclude the risk of using illegally logged timber while leaving options to use post-consumer recycled paper as well.

Dedication

To my lovely husband Roy, for all his unwavering love, support, and encouragement, and to my son, Peter

Acknowledgements

Owing to my unexpected blindness, I want to thank volunteers from MK Reader Service, Sue O'Connor and Mary Downes, for their invaluable help in assisting me to complete my book, and especial thanks to Annie Dutton for then undertaking all the numerous complications of bringing this novel to print.

I loved writing this book and hope that you as readers will enjoy reading it just as much.

*Although the characters and the story are mostly true, some fiction has been added and no real names have been used.

ONE

The elderly man clung tightly to the steering wheel as he peered through the rain-splattered windscreen at the many cars ahead of him on the busy A36 autoroute leading towards Belfort and Besançon. He dared a quick glance into his rear-view mirror to see if he was still being followed. Unfortunately, any vision through the car's rear window, as well as both the wing mirrors, was obscured by the driving rain and blinding headlights of the heavy motorway traffic behind; but he would have been surprised if he'd managed to evade his enemies.

He'd realised that there could be trouble ahead when he'd bumped into the man as he was leaving the bank in Strasbourg only four days ago. Looking up to apologise, his blood had run cold as he'd recognised the identity of the elderly man before him. At the same moment, the other man's pale blue eyes sharpened with a similar recognition.

'Hold on a minute. I know you, don't I? Karl Weiss?' the man had said, snapping out his query in German, hostility and suspicion tingeing his voice.

'No, no! You're mistaken!' he'd mumbled in French and slipped away as quickly as his old rheumatic joints would allow him. It had been necessary to make a trip to Strasbourg and it was an unlucky chance that he'd decided to visit the bank there before starting his journey back home to his apartment in the pleasant town of Besançon. After all these years – as each decade had passed, peacefully and uneventfully – he'd not really felt a need to be so watchful anymore. Now, however, it was obvious that the word had been passed on since his unfortunate encounter the other day, and his whereabouts had been discovered only too easily – even here in France. But why they were still bothering to seek him out so assiduously after all this time was extraordinary. And for what gain? For all they knew, he could already have profited from his little windfall long ago! But these people were acting as if they were in fact *aware* that he'd never found the opportunity – or the stomach – to do so.

Looking at the situation with hindsight, it was now obvious that, although he had had no suspicions at the time and been merely careful, someone must have tailed him back to his car in Strasbourg on that unfortunate day last week, and noted that it was an American vehicle and could be easily spotted. It appeared therefore that his pursuers had known exactly what they were looking out for and had obviously recognised the vehicle as he'd passed by, barely a week later, on his way back from an unavoidable trip to Colmar. Still always watchful for anything out of the ordinary, he'd soon realised he was being followed while still travelling on the A35 autoroute towards Basel and Switzerland. As he'd reached the junction of the two motorways, he had taken a sudden, last-second switch onto the A36 autoroute access lane, but so, too, he'd thought despairingly, had at least one of the vehicles he suspected was shadowing him, although it was difficult to judge in such difficult weather conditions.

Well, it was obvious now that he couldn't chance going home and risk leading these unknown people straight to his apartment. He felt a coldness fill him at his next thought: surely they hadn't managed to find his address yet? So soon?

His mind slipped back into the past. Until he'd bumped into the man last week in Strasbourg, he'd almost forgotten about the whole business. Thinking about it now, he could guess fairly accurately what these people must want, and was determined that they would fail. He then thought about the temptation he'd been faced with all those years ago when he was a tiny part of the invading German army in Greece during the Second World War. He'd watched all his superior officers plundering museums, houses, and shops and knew how and where they'd secreted all the wealth and artefacts – supposedly for the German Reich but mostly of course for their own profit. Although he had been just a lowly office clerk, he'd taken something for himself when he had been presented with the perfect opportunity, believing that no-one would be any the wiser, especially as they'd all known by then they were losing the war. It had been every man for himself in a quest for survival. But somehow his superior officers *had* found out.

Was he sorry now for the dangerous inheritance he'd gathered for his family? At the time, when the German army had disbanded in disarray knowing the war to be lost, he'd panicked and hidden his acquisitions locally, in Greece, fearful of being searched if they'd discovered his whereabouts. All he'd retained was a map he'd scribbled in a hurry, with codes to help him identify the hiding place. But by leaving his booty at a destination so distant from his home, he'd never really had the chance to return to collect – and therefore profit from – his ill-gotten gains. Truth to tell, he wished now he'd never yielded to temptation. But, for heaven's sake, he'd been not much more than a teenager then!

Once back in Germany after the war, he'd quickly decided to move across the border into France and start a new life. It was not long before he met and married his young wife and been welcomed into her large family near Besançon. It meant he'd had to leave behind his own few relatives, who lived in Germany, but fortunately his parents were already dead by then and he'd been an only child. As he had also taken the opportunity to change his second name to Weissmann when he'd arrived in France, as a further precaution, the French locals had believed he was a Jew, so he'd encountered more pity than hostility from his neighbours.

Ironically, during all those years since the war, fate seemed to have conspired to prevent him from revisiting Greece. Firstly, his wife had been too poorly for him to leave home, and then, later, his feckless son-in-law had deserted his daughter and her lovely child so it had been necessary for him to take them both back into the security of his own household. Then, somehow over the years, the whole thing seemed to lose its importance because his life seemed full and happy enough without the need to profit from items that were not his possessions in the first place.

What really puzzled the desperate driver was *why* he was still being sought so diligently – after all these years. After all, he'd only taken a few small, minor baubles! He frowned with puzzlement. Yes, he'd taken something that didn't belong to him – but so had they. All of them! He was no worse than they were. Yet he'd realised very soon after the war, that his former superiors in the army were still reaching out tentacles to locate him. That fact had frightened him sufficiently to cause him to plan a permanent home for himself in another country and had made it impossible to ever consider the idea of returning to live in Germany.

For the first time since the event all those years ago, he questioned if what he'd taken had been more important than he'd realised. Now, because of the ruthless chasing by his hunters, he suspected that this could be very much the case. Why else all this activity?

He remembered the time immediately after the war when he was still living in Germany. One of his ex-army companions, Klaus, had sought him out. They had seemingly met by coincidence in a local beer cellar, but in retrospect maybe the meeting had been contrived? When Klaus had led the conversation towards the stolen artefacts and claimed to have acquired a few trinkets for himself, he, Karl, had been unwise enough to be led into bragging about his little haul, too, and how he'd needed to draw a little map to help him eventually recover his items. They'd laughed about the possible problems of faulty or failing memories, and then Klaus had tried to lead him into revealing whereabouts he'd secreted his booty, but by then, he'd become suspicious of Klaus's motives. He had begun to wonder, for the first time, who it was he was he was working for, but had played along by agreeing to meet the man again the following week. Of course, he'd never intended to keep their date. He'd planned to disappear as quickly as possible, and within days had moved from Germany to France.

Until this moment he'd forgotten about Klaus, but now it all made sense – the people chasing him knew he owned a map, and had probably never destroyed it. He tried to recall just what he'd told his ex-colleague about the location of his modest haul. Had he told him that it was hidden on the Peloponnese peninsula in southern Greece? It was very likely that he had, although he was sure he'd not revealed the *exact* location of the hiding place – in the old ruins he'd encountered while on his desperate journey southwards towards the coast. Oh yes, he'd realised that anyone searching for him would have expected him to head for Athens, so he'd headed in the opposite direction, towards Kalamata! And his ruse had worked very well because he'd not been caught.

Another thought occurred to him. The pursuers chasing him today could not *all* be elderly – well, really quite old – like he was. The people concerned back then had been his seniors and surely not many of them could still be alive, although of course he knew at least one person who was. He thought again about the man he'd seen in the bank. Who were the others? Sons or other family members of the people he was involved with? Once again, he was overcome with a feeling of puzzlement and trepidation. Why would they bother so *much* to attempt to catch him of all people after all this *time*? There must be at least two cars chasing him tonight. The only explanation was that his earlier thoughts were correct. All those years ago – a lifetime – he really *had* taken something that all these people really wanted.

The frightened man turned his mind to the actual vehicle he was driving so wildly now. A friend of his had previously owned it and he had long admired it. When his friend had recently decided to sell the vehicle, he had been given first refusal. An American GMC Safari passenger van, imported into France, it had all the attributes that he needed if he were to go on a long trip – to Greece for instance. The seats converted easily into a bed, which was an important consideration.

There was also plenty of room for stowing all the necessities for camping. Now, if only he could lose his followers, he needed to utilise all these benefits. He desperately hoped they had not managed to locate his apartment as he definitely couldn't run the risk of leading them straight to his home. Although these days he lived alone – his wife had died just last year and his daughter had remarried and moved to Canada – it was his granddaughter he was worrying about. She or her husband often popped in to visit him and it was important not to involve them, especially if they were followed from there to their own home some twenty kilometres away. No, he would have to stay away for now and hope for the best. For a few minutes he allowed himself to think about his granddaughter. What a lovely girl she had grown to be, despite the desertion of her adored father. Thoughtful, kind, and beautiful, inside and out. And now she was married to a very good man she had known for years.

Bringing his thoughts back to the present, it occurred to him that perhaps he should have realised it was highly likely his vehicle would have been easily recognised – after all it was rather unusual. He needed now to plan his next move carefully. After a few moments of pondering, he decided to leave the autoroute further ahead, without prior warning, and turn towards Vesoul, an area he was familiar with, and try to lose his tail through the back lanes. Once he'd succeeded, he'd join the A6 autoroute and travel south, away from his home in Besançon, and find a campsite to stay on. The old man sighed heavily. The prospect of camping was not so pleasant now that his bones ached so much; he was really just too old for all this. But it would be much the safest option. He doubted they'd even *consider* the possibility that he was camping.

The old man reached his hand to the pocket inside his jacket and felt reassured to touch the envelope he was glad he'd been carrying with him for the last few days. It contained the battered old item which had been buried so deeply under more than fifty years of amassed possessions at his home that it had proved hard for him to locate it.

However, since his scare in Strasbourg, he felt better that he had kept the information close to him, although he hadn't expected to be traced so quickly, if at all. He'd taken the precaution of placing his precious document inside the envelope and had prepared it ready to send to his granddaughter in case of trouble. Now it was imperative that he should post this letter to her immediately. The bewildered old man cursed softly because all he needed was a stamp, but realised he didn't have any left in his wallet, and no Post Offices would be open at this time of night. Then, through the rapidly increasing darkness and the driving rain, he spotted a road sign advertising the next service area. Keeping his fingers crossed that it would be possible, he decided to purchase a pack of postage-prepaid envelopes in the shop. He'd quickly scrawl a note to his granddaughter, explaining what to do with the contents.

Five kilometres later he pulled in front of a large van and without signalling turned off into the approach lane for the service facility, desperately hoping his followers hadn't noticed. He drove past the fuel pumps, shops, and restaurant into the relative darkness beyond and looked for a suitable sheltered area to lose himself in. If he parked amongst ordinary vehicles, his higher-than-average van would stick out like a sore thumb. Then he saw what he was looking for – a space between a couple of the many lorries parked beyond the lines of cars – and gratefully swung his vehicle into the welcome shelter of the narrow gap between them.

Although he felt fairly optimistic that he'd accomplished his exit from the autoroute without being spotted, he decided, after thinking carefully, that it would be too risky to take the envelope with him now in case his followers *had* noticed and then subsequently attacked and searched him. Perhaps they were more observant and cleverer than he'd given them credit for. He would have to make his purchase, then if possible return to the vehicle, re-write his granddaughter's address on the new pre-stamped envelope, placing the old envelope plus its contents inside, and post the letter elsewhere. It would be foolhardy to post it here when it meant walking back to the rest area building again. Planning ahead, he thought that once he was on the back roads around Vesoul he would post his letter in the post box in the centre of Lure village. He knew exactly where that was.

Alternatively, he could just *destroy* the map, which would put an end to the whole miserable business. But if his small hoard *had* been something more significant – maybe really important – it would then stay hidden for evermore. No, that fact made it even more important to preserve the details and pass them to his beloved granddaughter for the time being. For now it was essential that he should hide the document. Knowing that for at least a few minutes he was safely out of view, he quickly pulled the tattered old envelope from his pocket, awkwardly climbed into the area between the second row of seats and felt carefully under one of them for the special hiding place he'd so recently prepared for such an eventuality. Feeling the edge of the small square of carpet, he slowly worked his gnarled, bony fingers under the area until he'd sufficiently lifted the section. Then he quickly pushed the envelope under the square and tamped the carpet back into place until it became smooth and flat again, and invisible.

With difficulty he collapsed back into his own seat, puffing with the effort of the climb and trying hard to control his breathing. He noticed that his whole body was trembling with tension – and fright – and he could feel his heart thumping away erratically. Attempting to calm himself, he made an effort to gather his thoughts for a minute or two. Now if they surprised him, he rationalised, there would be nothing on him to find, and he would tell them nothing! That wouldn't be difficult anyway, now his memory was failing. Without his document, he couldn't remember any of the details, apart from the facts that they were already aware of. However, they would rightly assume, or already knew, thanks to Klaus, that he'd drawn a map at the time to aid his memory, and still retained it. Smiling grimly, he thought, 'Oh, yes! X marks the spot all right! They'll be sorely disappointed if they've already searched my apartment. They will never guess that what they're looking for is hidden in my vehicle at this very moment.'

He would now move quickly to the shop and make his purchase. After that, if he were still convinced that he'd not been located, he'd come back, prepare his letter and drive like a madman until he reached the post box – *any* post box! Once that was done, he would be able to relax a bit, although he wondered what his granddaughter would make of the contents when she received the letter in a few days' time. He'd add a note warning her not to visit his home at any cost. If she was identified and followed back to her own home, he would have as good as handed his map straight to his enemies by posting it to her. Yes, that meant he should buy a writing pad as well. He'd ask her to hide the contents in a really safe place, and tell her that he'd explain everything to her when he returned.

If, later, he was sure that he'd managed to lose his followers, one plan could be to intercept the letter before his granddaughter opened it. He didn't *really* want her involved in this mess and any possible danger. After achieving that objective, maybe it would be a good time to disappear into Greece and see if his memory and his chart together would enable him to recover the objects he'd hidden there. This whole episode had brought back to him his unfortunate lapse of honesty, and perhaps the matter should now be dealt with, once and for all. Thank goodness he always carried a fair amount of cash and had all his credit cards in his pocket. Yes, that was a good plan!

What he would *really* like to do now more than anything was to return his spoils to the original owners, whoever they were. Could he actually do that, he wondered? Would they all understand that he'd been young and impressionable when he'd succumbed to temptation all those years ago. Being dragged into the war as a teenager had been a bad business. Since then he'd managed to put all that to the back of his mind and had lived his life well without profiting from his ill-gotten gains; to return the items would be a fitting end to the whole debacle, he felt.

He opened the car door, and was immediately splattered with rain as he slid awkwardly out onto uneven ground covered in large puddles. Around him the lights reflected dazzlingly on the wet surface, contrasting with the blackness beyond the well-lit area. His still-sharp blue eyes peered beyond the shelter of the lorries, but there was little chance he could identify if any of the parked or moving cars beyond were his pursuers. All he could do was carry out his purchases as speedily as possible and get back safely to his vehicle. As long as the lorry to his right didn't decide to leave, his van was completely out of sight to most areas of the parking complex.

The old man wrapped his coat closely around him and shivered as he splashed across the wetness of the parking area in an attempt to find the quickest route towards the welcoming lights of the large rest area building. While he was busily concentrating on avoiding the deepest puddles in an effort to keep his feet dry, he was unaware of the furtive movement of at least two people, almost invisible in the surrounding darkness, closing in towards him . . .

* * *

Lurking behind a clutch of lorries, the two young, shabbily dressed north-European men watched the American van pull in and park between two lorries towards the edge of the parking area. Their clothing was soaked through with the drenching rain as they examined the parked lorries in the hope of stowing away inside one of them. They were travelling north, but were not sure exactly where they were in France. Most of the lorries were firmly secured against thieves or stowaways, and none of them appeared to have plates that indicated they were heading northwards – Germany or Holland would have been good enough as their desired destination was Rotterdam. Most of the lorries parked there were Spanish, Italian, or Portuguese, and appeared to be heading towards Britain.

Creeping closer, they peered around the nearest lorry and

watched the van for a while. They were puzzled that such a vehicle had been parked so secretively between the lorries and wondered if the owner was hiding from someone. Eventually the driver's door opened and with difficulty an old man climbed out and moved slowly towards the main building, disappearing from view behind the obscuring curtain of heavy rain and early evening darkness.

'Did you see that? The old fool didn't lock his car! We'll take it and be across the border into Germany before it's even missed,' crowed the tallest man delightedly. 'It's a simpleton's job to start an engine like that without a key. Just watch me! Once we're in Rotterdam we can try to sell the van. If we can find a buyer, no questions asked, we'd be sure to make some money with such an unusual vehicle. If it's too difficult to sell, we'll just dump it!'

'More comfortable than cramped up in the back of a lorry,' agreed the other man. 'We can sleep in it and go wherever we want. Let's do it. At least we've got enough money to buy all the fuel we'll need.'

'Fast, then!' urged the first man. 'Let's be on our way.'

They moved rapidly towards the vehicle, peering furtively to see if there were any observant lorry drivers around to witness their actions. However, the darkness and the rain provided a dense screen, and the two figures, slipping silently through the shadows, concentrated on their objective – the theft of the unlocked American van.

TWO

The man, solidly built, of medium height, with very short, cropped, toffee-brown hair, stood outside his garage in the brightness of the spring afternoon. Being fair-skinned, he appeared younger than his actual age, and, although not particularly handsome, his broad lightly freckled face had a pleasant quirky expression with lips mostly curled upwards in a ready smile. He sighed with contentment as he regarded his recent purchase with satisfied eyes. He'd been searching the internet for some time for exactly the right vehicle. 'Hurrah for eBay!' he thought, because he'd spotted the American GMC Safari van as soon as it appeared on the website and had successfully bid for it. He'd been able to stay overnight with an old friend in Oldham, which had enabled him to arrive at the garage near Manchester early enough that morning to complete the purchase of the elderly vehicle and still arrive home just after midday. His vivid blue eyes sparkled with undisguised pleasure as he regarded his new acquisition.

He reflected that however miserable his life had been for the past few years, he had now acquired an object that could provide him with many hours not only of mechanical titivating, but a new interest, an absorbing hobby to pursue, and one which, in time, could provide a means of travelling cheaply – well, if not exactly *cheaply*, at least economically – across Europe on a variety of sightseeing trips.

Since his feckless wife had left him to live with a formerly so-called friend five years earlier, and taken their two sons with her, he'd been extremely unhappy and at a loose end. What a terrible blow it had been, he recalled, when, out of the blue, his wife had coolly informed him that she didn't love him anymore and wanted a divorce.

Just for a moment, he allowed a vision of his ex-wife, Pamela, to fill his mind. With a pert-featured face dominated by a pair of mischievous green eyes, all surrounded by a cloud of champagne-coloured curly hair, and a voluptuously curved body, she had been the first girl he'd ever had any serious feelings for, and he'd loved her passionately. Now he could visualise her image without any real emotion, except perhaps regret. And, yes, some resentment too at the callous way she'd betrayed him, feeding him a myriad of lies right up to the end. Although he was on reasonable terms with her these days – that much was necessary because she would always be the mother of his sons – he'd long ago lost any respect for her as a person, and once that point had been reached, all the love and passion he'd ever felt for her had gradually withered away.

Of course, the worst part of all had always been the loss of his boys. He hated being a 'MacDonald's Dad' on Saturdays, sitting amongst all the other dumped dads accompanied by children who always seemed to be treating their ex-parent more like strangers. Although he saw his boys most weekends, it wasn't the same as being part of the fabric of their lives. Being denied the role he loved – to be with and see his sons on an intimate, daily basis – had been the most devastating part of the whole miserable marriage break-up.

It was all still very traumatic and he'd gradually realised that he was tired of trying to compete with his ex-friend who was now the new 'Dad' in his children's lives. He was fighting a losing battle and, already, he felt that now the boys were growing older, they were both beginning to distance themselves from him, and had even started concocting excuses to avoid spending time with him, which he found very distressing and something he had absolutely no control over. Obviously preferring to being out and playing football with their friends or spending time on their computers, they seemed to be just performing a necessary duty when visiting him, rather than enjoying his company.

Now in his late thirties, Piers Smithieson, 'Perry' to all his friends, felt that he had now taken the first step towards building a new existence for his future. He had made a positive move towards a new and better life for himself – or at least something different – that would hopefully begin to banish all the remaining sadness. Once again, an image of his former life filled his mind – a happy day visiting an animal sanctuary, his two boys excitedly pointing out various creatures; he and Pamela arm in arm, with her smiling warmly as she slanted her gaze up towards him. He quickly shut down the image before it could adversely affect his present feeling of elation.

Once again, he turned his attention back to the present and congratulated himself on successfully obtaining this handsome vehicle. Then his eyebrows knitted together in a frown as he remembered something odd. Earlier, when he'd picked the car up at the garage, the owner told him that the previous evening he had been approached by two men who had offered him a higher figure than Perry had paid, if he would sell the van to them. He'd refused their offer and told them that, as far as he was concerned, the vehicle was already sold. Well, Perry had answered him, smiling, he couldn't blame someone else for wanting the Safari so badly. After all, they were rarely seen in this country!

'But they didn't want to take "No" for an answer,' the man had explained, looking rather uncomfortable. 'They were quite persistent, but I still told them that as far as I was concerned the van wasn't my property any longer and had already been sold – to you. I explained that you'd be collecting it the next day. Then they asked if they could look inside the vehicle, but once again I refused. They were foreigners – East European perhaps – and I didn't like their attitude at all!'

The garage owner had then hesitated, looking concerned, and had continued, 'I don't want to worry you, and it's probably not connected to your vehicle at all and just a weird coincidence, but there was a disturbance last night when someone tried to enter the compound. All I can say is that the lights and alarms must have frightened off the intruders before they succeeded in getting in!'

The man had obviously been spooked by this episode, and Perry had sensed that he'd probably felt a lot more threatened by the attitude of these people than he was prepared to admit to his customer. He had thanked the garage owner for his integrity in honouring their agreement, but feeling a bit edgy and bit spooked himself after this recent conversation, he'd been more watchful than normal of the traffic around him. He thought he'd noticed the same red car behind him several times on his journey from Manchester back to his home near Milton Keynes in Buckinghamshire, but then wondered if he was being paranoid in suspecting that someone was actually following him. Perhaps he was letting his imagination run away with him.

Now back at home, he began to wonder if perhaps something illegal had been hidden in the vehicle. The garage owner had informed him that he'd bought the vehicle from a Latvian who'd imported it into England, which was why the Safari had a brand-new logbook. Then he remembered that the garage owner had told him that the over-persuasive, would-be purchasers had been East Europeans. Could they have been Latvians? That would make sense, if they suspected that something had been inadvertently left inside the car. The thought that perhaps the Safari had been used for trafficking drugs or similar while abroad made Perry's blood run cold, and he hastily executed a panicky rummage throughout the vehicle.

Once he'd completed a thorough search into all the vehicle's nooks and crannies, his mind was soon put at rest. Sitting back on his haunches on the floor of the van and feeling the damp sheen of perspiration on his forehead, he took stock of his haul. All that had been revealed was nothing more significant than a foreign – probably Latvian – parking ticket, a few sheets of service history written in French that were some years old, some other papers, also French, concerning the vehicle's gas conversion, and some old sweet wrappers. The logbook identified the vehicle as only arriving in England during the last couple of months, so it certainly must have done the rounds abroad.

Putting any more fanciful ideas out of his head he concentrated on the happier prospect of how to 'pimp his ride'! He had already decided that three rows of seats in the vehicle was one row too many. Looking at the available space, he decided to remove the middle row so as to provide more room for some essential camping equipment. The rear seat dropped backwards and formed a reasonable-sized bed, which would be more than adequate for him to sleep on.

During the evening, he decided that working on the Safari would be a lot more interesting than staring at the television, so he wandered outside into the residual warmth of the late April evening and, collecting his toolbox from the garage, set about releasing the bolts under the surplus seats. About an hour later he triumphantly lifted them free from the interior. The carpet throughout the vehicle was fairly worn in the expected places, but where it had lain under the unwanted seats it was clean and as good as new. He absent-mindedly smoothed his hand over the carpet pile, his lively brain already calculating his next job. As he did so he felt something uneven catch his skin. Looking sharply at the surface, he could see that an almost invisible square had been cut into the carpet and then squeezed smoothly back into position; it would have been impossible to see with the seats still fixed in their original location.

His heart sank as he considered what horrors he might find. Perhaps after all there were still some drugs hidden inside; the men in Manchester had obviously been very keen to search the car's interior. Almost reluctantly, yet paradoxically consumed with curiosity, he carefully worked his fingers under the removable square of carpet until it came free on three sides. After carefully folding it back, he heaved a sigh of relief when he discovered that there was no special cavity fitted underneath, just the normal floor surface. As he looked a second time, however, he could see a crumpled piece of paper pushed almost out of sight under the main carpet. Edging the paper free, he saw that it was an old envelope, which, when he turned it over, was addressed to someone in France. The writing was a beautifully formed script – not at all like the scribbles of most people today, if they even wrote letters!

With the envelope in his hand and still in shock at his discovery, his horrified eyes quickly swept the road nearby for any strange vehicles – especially red cars. The last thing he wanted was for anybody to actually *witness* his success in finding what was an extremely well-hidden object. That was the best thing about his house being in a cul-de-sac; any strange car around would stick out like a sore thumb. He relaxed. There was no suspicious vehicle lurking nearby or, indeed, anybody watching him at all.

He turned his attention again to the envelope, which was unsealed, and found inside a small folded sheet of paper, dog-eared and tattered. After carefully extracting it from the envelope and smoothing it flat, his sharp blue eyes narrowed as he gazed at the tiny hand-scrawled map in front of him. He racked his brains in an effort to work out the possible location indicated by the drawing. Studying the name written down, he would guess it was somewhere in Greece. 'Mystras' was mentioned, and the name tugged at his memory. Was that somewhere his parents had taken him on one of their trips to Greece? He'd been a teenager then and still had some memories of visiting one of the many historic areas that had been particularly beautiful, set on a hillside with wonderful panoramic views. He'd have to check the atlas but he would guess that Mystras was somewhere on the Peloponnese, which he remembered was technically an island, being divided from the Greek mainland by the Corinth Canal.

Perry started to worry. It seemed fairly obvious to him now that this envelope must have been what someone had been hoping to find if they'd had a chance to search the vehicle. In that case, if he'd any sense at all, he'd replace the envelope, leave the carpet square uneven and obvious to anyone looking – and leave the Safari unlocked for a while! If he was right, the vehicle would soon be accessed, the envelope taken, and that would be that.

He bit his lip thoughtfully, and stared again at the tattered map. He was intrigued to find out what it signified and felt strangely reluctant to follow his own advice. Suppose instead he attempted to deliver the letter to the address in France and maybe find out why it was hidden so carefully? But how many years had it been tucked away under the carpet? Perhaps the person had moved in the meantime. Nonetheless, he decided, if he did anything at all, it would be his *duty* to at least attempt to find the intended recipient and present the letter and map to them. But what if that proved completely impossible? Maybe, then, he could continue on to Greece – to Mystras. Not only could he enjoy a holiday, but he could also attempt to unravel the mystery of the old map.

What bothered him, though, was supposing he did set out on the journey, would he still find himself being followed? He thought he had already seen a red car, similar to the one that had followed him on the M1 motorway, driving slowly down the close where he lived, soon after he'd arrived home. Or was he simply being too suspicious? After all, there were millions of red cars on the roads and one of his neighbour's visitors owned a similar red vehicle. Still, some spirit of caution had made him resist an earlier impulse to travel to his small office and storage unit on a nearby industrial estate to collect more tools. So, he was now coming to the uncomfortable conclusion that if this item proved to be what these people were looking for, they probably wouldn't rest until they had found it.

For some moments he pondered the problem, and then a brilliant idea began to take shape in his head! Suddenly he felt an unaccustomed sense of excitement fill his body as he considered his plan, because unexpectedly the whole situation now seemed to present itself not as an uncomfortable situation but, rather, as a challenge – a game to be played – and won! No, not just a game, more like an adventure. He'd fake up another map of somewhere completely different and place it in an envelope addressed to a fictitious address in France – not of course to the destination of the original map. He would have to 'age' it to a similar scruffy appearance, and when he 'hid' his new creation, the square of carpet would have to be not quite as carefully tamped back into place – just visible enough to catch the eye of anybody searching carefully. If he were just being fanciful, then the envelope would stay undisturbed in its secret hiding place, but if he was right in his suspicions, the envelope would soon disappear and the searchers would be content to leave him, and the Safari, alone. He felt again a delightful thrill of determination to fool any searchers and trick them into believing they'd succeeded in their attempts: if indeed there were any searchers. He was still not really sure if it was just a figment of his suspicious mind. Time would tell, he concluded.

Feverishly searching amongst his possessions, Perry came across an old exercise book with a few empty pages that were yellowed with age and torn at the edges. Perfect! Still refusing to take the situation completely seriously, he rather enjoyed faking the new item. He debated with himself as to the location of the target for his offering, and eventually settled on another region in Greece, to render more genuineness to the map. After referring to a reference book about the ruins at Delphi on the Greek mainland, he drew a rough plan of the whole layout, and then indicated the target location in the building that had been the treasury or counting house on the higher side of the access road. After adding some symbols and squiggles that he hoped would seem meaningful, and placing the finished product in a battered old envelope he'd discovered at the back of a drawer, he then added the fictional address and name of a woman in the area of Saint Denis, Paris, as authentic as he could concoct, using a scratchy old biro. He was more than satisfied with the results, and decided that it should keep the people who were possibly after him busy for a while – at least as long as his bogus map continued to resemble what they were searching for.

It was imperative, he thought, to insert his masterpiece into the cleverly concealed hiding place before going to bed. If his van was searched that very night, the hiding place discovered and no contents found, the whole plan would have failed. It would also lead any searchers to assume rightly that Perry had definitely discovered the hiding place himself once he'd removed the centre row of seats. That was the last thing he wanted.

* * *

Only two days later Perry discovered that the envelope he'd so carefully prepared with the fake map and different address *had* been removed. He had been leaving the vehicle unlocked overnight, as if by accident, and as it was parked on his drive with his other car, a small Corsa, parked behind it to block it in, he'd deemed that nobody could actually steal the vehicle itself.

Perry was filled with a sense of feverish excitement when he realised that his assessment had been correct all along, and that someone *had* actually been searching for the map. He rapidly made his plans. It was now a matter of urgency to remove the vehicle from sight and change its appearance as radically as possible. He was fairly confident that unless his pursuers realised more quickly than he expected that the map was a fake, they would not be watching his movements for at least a few days.

Perry was a self-employed plumber/electrician and until recently had been very successful and busy. However, only a year ago he had been very lucky with a win on the lottery – not millions, but still a cool three-quarters of a million! This had enabled him to purchase his present home, a modest two-bedroom house with attached garage. Apart from that expenditure, he had not touched the rest of his savings. Now it was just the right time to take a break, he rationalised, especially while his workload was so light. He'd not had a holiday for years – since before his divorce, in fact – so now was the ideal time to go away and try out his van's capabilities.

Firstly, he'd see if he could stay with his friend, Andy, who owned a farm near Cheltenham in Gloucestershire. While there he could spray the vehicle a different colour and then add some exterior accessories such as a bicycle rack. The lower half of the vehicle was a royal blue colour, and Perry decided to spray that section a dark silver. While he was at Andy's he would also change the number plate and replace it with a 'cherished' registration that he could buy on-line. Surely all those changes would successfully ensure that the vehicle would not be recognised by the people who might decide to pursue him again at some point. He'd already decided that if it proved impossible to deliver the map to the rightful owner, he would definitely continue on to Greece and see if he could make any sense of the scribbled instructions. If he did carry out this plan, the last thing he wanted was for the people, maybe also in Greece having realised the map was a fake, recognising his van as he drove past them by sheer chance. Changing the vehicle altogether was not an option; he had been searching too long to let it go now. It wasn't an option either to use his little Corsa as it had a tendency to be unreliable as well as being limited on storage space for such a long journey.

That evening, in the security of his own property, he examined the original envelope carefully. The letter was addressed to a Madame Etienne N, Maison le Lauriers, Challigny, Langueres. After studying a road atlas of France for some time, he eventually found the tiny village of Challigny. It lay some twenty or more kilometres north-north-west of Besançon and halfway between there and the town of Chaumont. After turning down the corner of the appropriate page in his atlas, ensuring that he could find the place more easily the next time he wanted to check his route, he sat in thought, a glow of excitement and curiosity filling his body. He knew where he had to go now, and he wondered what reception he'd receive when he tried to deliver the envelope in person. Would the woman be old, or maybe younger with a bevy of young children around her? He'd have to be patient for a while longer yet, that was certain.

However, impatient as he was to set off, he first had a phone call to make. He picked up his telephone and tapped out a familiar number.

He heard a click as the receiver was lifted at the other end.

'Hi, Sheila! I wondered if it would be okay for me to come and stay with you for a few days? Yes? Oh, brilliant! Could I come as early as tomorrow, if it's convenient? I know it's short notice but I do have my reasons. Oh, good! Right, I'll look forward to seeing you two tomorrow then. I've got a lot of things to tell you both!'

THREE

Perry had parked on the main street of the small village of Challigny, outside a *boulangerie* so his presence would not look suspicious. Sitting comfortably in his van, he had already taken the opportunity to grab something to eat from the shop and was chewing happily on a fresh baguette filled with ham and salad. At the same time, he carefully observed the shabby brown front door of the tall house on the opposite side of the road.

The small garden fronting the property was filled with colourful, newly-opened oleander buds, unable any longer to resist the warmth of the spring sun's coaxing heat, creating vivid splashes of colour that contrasted spectacularly with the rather dreary exterior of the house. He had already walked along the path to the front door, rung the bell and discovered that there was no one at home. The lady behind the counter in the *boulangerie* had, however, kindly informed him that the occupant was likely to be back very shortly with her daughter.

Staring along the pavement, he espied a dumpy woman with a small child firmly clutching her hand walking along the pavement. As they turned into their gate, Perry jumped out of his car and hastened across the road towards them.

'Excusez mois, madame!' he called in his best French. *'Il chercher pour Madame Etienne!'*

Hoping the poor woman would understand his inaccuracies, he experienced a twinge of disappointment as she turned to face him. She had a homely, though not unpleasing appearance, but he had imagined his quarry to be younger and more attractive – irrational really, because there was no logic to his expectations, only a wishful thinking! In careful English she said, 'Madame Etienne not 'ere anymore.'

'So,' Perry thought, 'this isn't Madame Etienne after all!'

The little woman continued, 'She is gone for per'aps five years now. I regret I do not 'ave new address.' Observing Perry's crestfallen expression, she added, 'Madame 'ad job. She was teacher at l'école primaire Saint Cecilia in Langueres. She 'ad friends there. You should visit the school and talk to 'er friends.'

She paused, eyeing him curiously, then added confidingly, 'But I know that once 'er 'usband 'ad died, she wanted to move very quickly.'

The young child beside the woman shifted restlessly and stared hard at Perry with dark assessing eyes.

'*Merci Madame pour votre patience!*' Perry's hopes were again raised at the prospect of another source of information. He suspected he must now be searching for an elderly grieving widow – unless of course she'd formed a new relationship during the intervening years. Quickly dismissing that likelihood, he formed a new picture in his imagination of a rather sad, middle-aged, frumpy individual, rather like one of his past schoolteachers that he could still remember.

'*Je vous en prie* – you are welcome, monsieur. I am sorry you are disappointed.' With that, the woman turned away and entered the house with her young daughter, leaving Perry standing among the colourful oleanders. Returning to his vehicle, pondering over what he had learned, he decided to wait until the next day to visit the school.

* * *

L'école Saint Cecilia was a school for younger children and was easy enough to find on the outskirts of the town of Langueres, although the playground was eerily quiet. Perry had decided to visit the school towards midday on the premise that Madame Etienne's teacher friends would be available to talk to him during the long break period. Joining a small group of women of all ages, he stood outside the locked gate; almost immediately a group of children accompanied by a young male teacher approached. He unlocked it and allowed the children to pass through to their waiting mothers – or surely grandmothers in some cases. Before he turned and started to walk back, the teacher observed Perry with curious, slightly hostile eyes, immediately identifying him as a stranger. Perry felt awkward as he stared back at the suspicious expression on the man's face; it indicated only too clearly that a stranger hanging around a school full of young children was not welcome.

'*Excusez mois, Monsieur! Je cherche pour les amis de Madame Etienne!*' he called nervously, hoping his attempt at French would be understood. He heaved a sigh of relief when the teacher walked back to the gate.

'You are Engleesh?' he asked. Perry confirmed that he was, and the teacher, speaking with a strong accent, replied, 'Madame Etienne was a teacher here until she moved from the area. I think it is Madame Bissières that you wish to speak to. She was the best friend of Madame Etienne.' As he was talking, he unlocked the gate and gestured for Perry to enter the school area.

'You must wait until lunch is finished to speak to Madame Bissières but you may wait over there. I will tell her to come to you.' The teacher pointed to a wooden seat set under a shady tree in the school grounds, and Perry resigned himself to a long wait. After what seemed an endless time, the decibels in the playground increased alarmingly as youngsters, now refuelled with quantities of nourishing food, shrieked and shouted as they romped and frolicked and were obviously making the most of their freedom after being cooped up in their classrooms.

Perry saw a young woman walking towards him.

'My name is Madame Bissières. I understand that you wish to speak to me about Madame Etienne?' she said rather curtly as she reached him.

Madame Bissières was a thin, pale-faced, sharp-featured woman, probably in her mid-thirties who, along with her male colleague, spoke rather better English than he spoke French. She seemed rather wary of his presence and the enquiries he was making about her friend, until

Perry introduced himself and explained about the strange letter he had found in his vehicle and that he just wanted to deliver the letter in person. Thereafter, she became much more friendly.

'Call me Sophie,' she invited Perry, and then settled down on the seat next to him to explain the situation.

'For some time Nathalie 'as wished to keep 'er address secret. She 'ad felt that her life could be in danger, but did not 'ave the reason why. She 'as no money or other possessions that anybody could wish to acquire, but strange things 'ave happened in 'er life that there was no explanation for.'

Noting Perry's puzzled expression, she added in her attractively accented English, 'Firstly 'er grandfather was killed – stabbed – in an autoroute service area not so far from 'ere, and his vehicle stolen at the same time. And then, shortly after, 'er 'usband was murdered too. After Nathalie's grandfather's tragic death, 'er 'usband 'ad been visiting the grandfather's apartment and sorting out 'is – what do you say – effects?' Perry nodded in confirmation and she continued, 'The police think 'e surprised a robber – a burglar.'

Sophie sighed and then continued, 'That is not all! At the time that all this 'appened, four – no, five – years ago, Nathalie 'ad been pregnant, but the shock of all these dreadful events caused 'er to miscarry. It was a very sad time for 'er, and all of us too.'

Perry, shocked by this information, suddenly felt a cold draught of danger overtaking what had been a mood of looking forward to and setting out on an interesting and mysterious adventure. The people following him had already *killed* two people who had got in their way! Could these really be the same people? The whole thing now seemed too complicated to fully absorb.

He also banished his present image of Madame Etienne from his mind. Pregnant? This woman could not, therefore, have been an elderly, frumpy teacher! Another image formed in his imagination of a thin, sad-faced, grieving woman who'd been a victim of an awful tragedy, her long face ravaged by the suffering and loneliness she'd been forced to endure after losing her nearest and dearest.

Sophie stared hard at Perry's face, which he hoped didn't mirror his present fear and confusion. She asked, 'You tell me you found an envelope inside your car. What car is it?'

Swallowing his misgivings, Perry answered proudly, 'An American GMC Safari multi-purpose vehicle. If you look over there you can see it beyond the railing!' He pointed, and then noted his companion's sharp intake of breath. 'You look shocked!' he commented.

'I am … surprised. I now see 'ow it was that you found an envelope inside. I think that could be the car that belonged to Nathalie's grandfather! The police were never able to trace it at the time and believed it 'ad been stolen and driven to another country!' After staring hard at the vehicle, she looked doubtful. 'Perhaps it is only similar. After all, I recall the car that Nathalie's grandfather owned was a different colour.'

Perry hastily explained that he'd resprayed the lower part of the vehicle and that the original colour had been bright blue.

'Yes!' Sophie exclaimed. 'I remember that it was blue and white. It truly must be the same car. Nathalie will be amazed to see it. That is, if you still intend to deliver the envelope?' The teacher paused, staring hard at Perry with speculative eyes. Then her body relaxed as she appeared to come to a decision.

'Nathalie wishes her address to be confidential, but I believe you are truthful and mean her no harm. For you to deliver the envelope it is of course necessary for you to know where she is. She now 'as a new 'ome in the area Haute Marne, which is perhaps fifty kilometres from 'ere, south-east of Tournus. The village is called Saint Armand and 'er 'ouse is called *Genevrière*. You will find it close to the centre of the village, in a road just off the main street called Rue Julien. I will telephone Nathalie and tell 'er that you may arrive very soon.'

Perry's pen quickly scribbled across an old envelope he'd found in his pocket as he attempted to capture all the information that Sophie was giving him.

'Thank you, Sophie, for all your help. Does Nathalie still live alone or has she remarried during this time?' he asked curiously.

'No, Nathalie 'as been living quietly – too quietly, to be truthful! She 'as become an 'ermit since all this 'appened, and perhaps your visit will be good for 'er!' Sophie sighed. 'She is still very un'appy because she does not understand why the two people she loved more than anyone in the world were taken from her. It is a conundrum that 'as been 'aunting her all these years.'

* * *

It was mid-afternoon and Perry found himself waiting outside a small neat house in a quiet side road near the centre of the large village of Saint Armand for his loud knock on the heavy wooden front door to be answered. As he listened to the twitterings of the martins nesting high above in the eaves, he recalled all the helpful information that Sophie had passed onto him and felt curious to meet this poor sad widow. Consequently, he was staggered as he came face to face with a lovely woman with long bouncy curls of bright auburn hair, clear fair skin and warm hazel eyes, who opened the door to him. Her eyes shrewdly assessed her rather comically discomposed visitor, approved of his appearance and quickly made a decision that this person would prove no threat to her safety. After all, Sophie had obviously formed a good opinion of him, and she trusted her friend's judgement.

'*Bonjour*, Madame Etienne, my name is Piers Smithieson – Perry – and your friend Madame Bissières gave me …' he stammered like a gauche schoolboy, staring with incredulous eyes at the beautiful calm face of the woman looking quizzically at him.

'It's fine! Sophie telephoned and told me to expect you,' Nathalie replied in English, her rather sad mouth curving into a welcoming smile.

'Please come inside. Would you like some coffee?' Then her eyes widened as she espied the vehicle parked against the kerb outside her property. 'That was my grandfather's vehicle?' Her voice faltered and she struggled to gain control of her emotions. 'It looks different to how I remembered it.'

As Perry followed Nathalie into the cool darkness of the hall, he answered her question. 'I believe it must have belonged to him, but, as I told your friend Sophie, I've made quite a few changes to its appearance . . . you speak English very well.'

Nathalie smiled again. 'I need to – I'm a teacher of English! Well I was, but I haven't been working since . . .' She tailed off wondering just how much Perry already knew about her life.

'I do know about your terrible experience. I hope you don't mind that Sophie filled me in with the broad details. All I can say is that I'm so sorry for your devastating loss.'

Nathalie turned away but not before Perry had seen her distress.

'Please don't be too sympathetic or I'll dissolve into a mess of tears! I'll go and make some coffee and by that time I will have recovered my courage and composure. After all, this happened more than five years ago.'

Once they were settled in Nathalie's comfortable sitting room, Perry told Nathalie about the letter he'd found, and where it had been hidden. He rummaged around in his jacket's inside pocket and produced the old envelope. As he handed it to Nathalie, he said, 'I'm afraid I'm guilty of looking inside the envelope as it wasn't sealed. Does that map inside mean anything to you, Madame Etienne?'

'Oh, please call me Nathalie!'

'I will as long as you agree to call me Perry.'

For two or three minutes, the young woman scrutinised the envelope and its contents with a perplexed expression. 'It means nothing to me,' she said, 'although the writing is my grandfather's, so he must have also drawn the map. Is it a place in Greece?'

'I believe it's a map of an old historic city called Mystras, which is near Sparta on the Peloponnese part of the mainland. Well, it's really an area divided from the mainland by the Corinth Canal, which makes it technically an island. I think I only recognise the place on the map because my parents dragged me around the area as an ungrateful surly teenager!' Perry admitted with a wry smile.

Nathalie laughed, and Perry admired the sparkle in her eyes and curve of her mouth. He guessed that she'd not had too much to laugh about over the past five years.

He added more seriously, 'I believe this map had great significance for your grandfather. It was something he needed to commit to paper because he suspected that his memory would fail him over the years, and it was something he wanted to pass to you for safe-keeping. And when that failed, he hid it in his vehicle. Do you know if he ever visited Greece, or is he only recording something he'd been told about?'

Nathalie shifted uncomfortably. 'He was in the German army during the Second World War, when Greece had become an occupied country. Yes, he was *German* – and I'm sure that was the only time he was in Greece! The fact that he was German was supposed to be a family secret, but over the years I'd heard enough bits and pieces to come to this conclusion. He must have been a very young man then, not much more than a teenager. It was immediately after the war when he moved to France and …'

'And what?'

'I'm not sure about this, but I believe he changed his name from Weiss to Weissmann when he came to France. I vaguely remember seeing that name written on something in his room when I was a lot younger. When I asked him about the name difference, he gave me some garbled explanation. His early life was almost a taboo subject. I believe he burnt a lot of his old documents after that. He used to make a joke about committing his past life to ashes!'

Perry sat still, digesting this last important fact. Had Nathalie's grandfather been so afraid of being pursued all those years ago that he'd changed his *name*?'

He said, 'You're really so certain that he'd never revisited Greece since then?'

'I'm positive he didn't. Someone in the family would have mentioned or referred to it if he'd been on a journey that far distant. Surely, also, he wouldn't have still been carrying the map around with him if he'd been back there to carry out whatever he'd needed to do. And anyway, my grandmother was sick for years before she died and needed looking after, and then, after my father deserted my mother when I was a young child, we both went to live with him. He really had his work cut out looking after his family!'

Perry nodded. 'So it doesn't seem very likely.'

'Still, I suppose I can't rule out the possibility,' Nathalie said slowly. 'How can we be entirely sure that, if something was hidden, my grandfather didn't recover whatever it was from that place years ago?'

Perry said thoughtfully, 'I think you were right in the first place. For a start, he wouldn't have still kept the map so close to him if he'd been back there, because he wouldn't have needed it anymore. And anyway, if he *had* accomplished whatever he'd wanted to do, why would anybody still be pursuing him as recently as just five years ago? The people chasing him obviously believed he hadn't been able to recover whatever it was he'd hidden. I wonder how that could be?' After a moment he added, 'Would it have been so obvious to all and sundry if he *had* done so? It's all very curious and I would really like to get to the bottom of the mystery!'

They chatted comfortably about themselves, their very different lifestyles, politics, fashions, hobbies; the conversation flowed easily on all subjects. They seemed more like two people who'd known each other for many years than strangers who'd only just met. Suddenly Perry realised that a couple of hours had slid past without him being aware of how long he'd been imposing his presence on this attractive girl with her sparkling hazel eyes, and brilliantly coloured hair that so perfectly framed the piquancy of her face.

'I'm sorry!' he exclaimed. 'You must have many things to do, and I've taken up so much of your time!'

Casting an oblique glance at him, Nathalie said quietly, 'I've enjoyed your company and there is not really so much in my life to fill my time. Would you care to stay for dinner with me here? Or we could visit a small restaurant I know nearby?'

Hardly believing his luck, Perry gratefully accepted the invitation that would enable him to spend a whole evening with this lovely but rather sad young woman.

* * *

Before long, the couple were comfortably ensconced in an intimate, private corner of the little local restaurant. After they'd almost worn themselves out with questions and answers about each other's lives, Nathalie finally asked Perry a question that was more difficult to reply to. 'If you hadn't been able to find me and deliver the envelope and map, what would you have done?' she enquired curiously.

Leaning back in his chair, Perry sighed and admitted slowly, 'To be really honest, I was planning to travel onwards to Greece and see if *I* could find what your grandfather had hidden, or at least discover why he'd gone to all the trouble to draw the map. But my guess is I would probably not have been successful. Don't even ask what I'd have done if I *had* found anything! I hadn't got that far in my thoughts. But I must admit I'm really curious to see what he hid that he obviously considered was worth saving.'

After a moment's silence, Nathalie surprised herself by crying out impulsively, 'Let's *both* go to Greece! Could I come with you? I've got nothing to stop me going and I'm sure it would be what my grandfather would want me to do!'

Swallowing his shock (and pleasure) at this unexpected

suggestion, Perry said regretfully, after an embarrassed silence, 'My vehicle is not really suitable to share, I'm afraid, because I'm planning to sleep in it. Especially so because we're strangers! And although it doesn't seem like it to me – we really *are*, and have only just met each other! Things would be a bit too … intimate …' He tailed off awkwardly.

'Oh, I'm so sorry! To make such a suggestion is an imposition!' cried Nathalie, her cheeks pink with mortification. 'Yes, indeed we *are* strangers, and I can only apologise for my crazy idea!'

'No, no!' replied Perry hastily, 'I think it's a *great* idea and I would *love* you to join me!' Looking at the uncertain expression on her face, he gripped her arm in an attempt to convince her of his sincerity. 'Let's face it, you've more right to make the trip than me – it's *your* adventure really. I was only thinking about camping and the sleeping arrangements and so on …'

'Oh! I have a new thought! That shouldn't be a problem, because I have a very good tent!' cried Nathalie with renewed excitement. 'If I can *travel* with you, I can use my tent for the nights. I have all the necessary equipment too. Bernard and I often used to go camping, here in France as well as to Italy and Austria!' She, too, tailed off, her eyes misting as she remembered the happy holidays she and her husband had enjoyed together before his cruel death.

With all the accommodation problems solved, the couple stared at each other with a growing excitement as they imagined the wonderful adventure ahead of them that would now be possible to share.

After a few quiet moments, Nathalie turned to Perry and touched his hand. She asked quietly, 'Do you think we could be in any danger if we do this?'

'I can't truthfully answer that,' replied Perry, 'but I do believe there are still people in England, the ones who tried to search the van, before and after I had bought it, who still want this map. If they are the same people that were after your grandfather, we have to remember that they've killed twice already. Having said that, I've every reason to feel that they've got no idea where I am now or what I plan to do.'

He went on to tell Nathalie how someone had tried to outbid the garage owner for the vehicle and the subsequent attempted break-in at the garage car pound. Although he'd been hoping the information wouldn't frighten Nathalie, he heard her gasp with shock as she absorbed the information. He went on to tell her how he suspected he'd been followed from the garage to his home, and then how he'd hidden a fake map in the same place he'd found Nathalie's grandfather's map.

'I'd already removed the second row of seats, which made the hiding place much easier to find. I left the vehicle unlocked at different times, and after a while I realised the fake map had gone!' he told her.

Nathalie looked horrified at first at this ominous piece of news, and then she chuckled. 'That was really clever of you. And now somebody will be looking in entirely the wrong place. I hope it's far enough away from the true hiding place.'

'Well, although I didn't take the matter too seriously at the time, I decided it still had to be somewhere in Greece to be believable, but I fastened on an area around the ruins of Delphi, which is on the mainland and further north than the Peloponnese, which is where we'll be going.'

Another thought occurred to Nathalie. 'Do you have any worries that the vehicle will be recognised by these … people? They know the American model and age of the vehicle, and, as you said, they recognised it at the time you purchased it.'

Perry smiled. 'You had a job to recognise it, didn't you? I've made a lot of changes to its overall appearance, applied for a new registration and added enough accessories to make it appear very different to the vehicle I bought.'

Nodding in agreement, Nathalie's face became serious as she said thoughtfully, 'My grandfather must have been sought out, found, and killed for the information contained on this map. It all makes sense now.

But he didn't tell them anything and they didn't find the map.'

'Surely they must have searched his car at that time as well, and yet, if they had, why are they *still* trying to search the interior?' Perry was puzzled.

Excitedly, Nathalie cried, 'His car disappeared on the same night! The police treated the two incidents as separate because a lorry driver had reported witnessing two shabby individuals hanging around the lorries and had thought at the time that they were looking for an opportunity to stow away in the back of the right vehicle! Just suppose *someone else* stole the vehicle at that time and my grandfather's murderers couldn't find it? You said it turned up in – Latvia – was it?'

'Yes. If the vehicle had been stolen, and the killers had then searched your grandfather's apartment and come up with nothing, that would have meant that anything important must have been hidden in the Safari. They'd have been almost sure, or even knew, that your grandfather *had* drawn a map of the burial site to refresh his memory. But they'd lost sight of the vehicle and didn't have any idea of where to search. They'd probably just about given up hope when someone must have seen it up for sale in Manchester via the internet. That would explain why the vehicle became so attractive to someone, but it was too late because I'd already paid for it!'

Nathalie's eyes misted. 'Bernard must have surprised these people while they were searching my grandfather's apartment. So they killed him too, stabbed him to death.' The blunt statement hovered in the air, the brutal baseline for the whole enterprise. She put her head in her hands and cried with anguish, 'My God, whatever did my grandfather hide that was so *important!*'

After a few minutes, when Nathalie had regained her composure, Perry stated, 'Well, one thing seems to be apparent – these people don't know anything about *your* existence! If they had, you would have been approached a long time ago.'

'My grandfather never left any personal information around his home. I used to find this strange and teased him about it once. He told me that he had committed to memory the only addresses that mattered. Then, after he was killed, and Bernard too, I took what I needed and went to stay with Sophie.' Nathalie sighed, and taking in the question on Perry's face, she admitted, 'I never went back to our house because I had this strange sense of danger. The removal people packed up everything for me and put it all into storage. It's still there, because I bought new furniture for this house.'

Perry asked carefully, 'You told me your grandfather was killed in an autoroute service area. Do you know why he was there, or if he felt threatened in any way?'

Nathalie put her hands to her face while she tried to remember the events of five years earlier. 'He was seen by another lorry driver, who was just leaving the area, parking out of sight between the two lorries immediately in front of him. His opinion was that my grandfather was hiding himself.'

'Um.' Perry thought for a moment and then asked, 'Do you know why your grandfather stopped in the service area? Did he buy anything?'

'Yes. Apparently he bought a pack of postage-prepaid envelopes. Oh, and a writing pad. Both items were found in his pocket, unused.'

Thinking this through, Perry pointed out, 'There's no stamp on the original letter, is there? Perhaps things had become urgent and he'd needed to post the map to you immediately. Without any stamps, he'd have needed to enclose the map in a prepaid envelope maybe? And he'd hidden the map in the vehicle in case he was intercepted while making his purchase, as indeed he was. It makes some sense. It must have been a blow to his pursuers if, as it seems, someone actually pinched the vehicle from under their very noses. Especially as, by the time they'd realised what they'd wanted wasn't in his apartment, it only left his vehicle as the hiding place. How ironic!'

Still upset by Nathalie's distress, Perry attempted to turn the conversation back to their projected journey, and they began to make some constructive plans for their departure. He observed the return of the sparkle in Nathalie's eyes and an upward curve to her shapely lips, and realised that, whatever might happen, this project would be good for her and could help her come to terms with her tragic past. Being honest, he also recognised that it would make the trip far more appealing to himself, too!

By the time the couple left the restaurant it was very late, but they were so involved with their plans that neither of them was aware of the time, or had noticed the hovering waiters hoping to close up for the night; they would not have cared anyway!

FOUR

Two weeks slipped by before they eventually finalised their arrangements and set off for what they both felt was going to be an exciting trip.

Stocked up with all the necessary supplies, they accomplished the rather tedious trek through Italy to the port of Brindisi, where it had been very easy to book the ferry crossing to Patras, the large port on the north-western edge of the Peloponnese island. While travelling through France and Italy, the weather had proved to be rather unsettled, but as they had travelled further south the climate improved greatly.

After studying the map, both Perry and Nathalie had decided that this route was safer than taking the more direct route and crossing from Venice to Igoumenitsa, because driving south from that port in north-west Greece would take them a tad too close to the area indicated on the fake map that Perry had drawn. In addition, there was a good chance that should their hunters decide to follow the map, they would almost certainly choose to travel to Igoumenitsa.

They found a pleasant campsite near the town of Pyrgos on the west coast and, totally beguiled by the warmth of the sun and the incredible deep-blue of the sea, they decided to stay for a few days while they finalised the details of their next move. There was an access path leading from the site to the sun-bleached sandy beach, so the two weary travellers were only too glad to take advantage of the early summer sunshine, although for them the sea was still rather too chilly for bathing. The panorama of vivid blue sea contrasted with the backdrop of mountains shaded in greens and mauves, dotted with white properties on the lower slopes, and larger villages providing a bigger splash of colour here and there, enchanted both the visitors equally.

As Perry glanced at the woman lying on the sand next to him, clad in a skimpy black swimsuit, and lying comfortably on her towel as she relaxed and basked in the warmth of the Greek sunshine, he couldn't help but admire the long curves of her shapely limbs, her trim waist and the marvellous swelling of her breasts. His eyes caressed the tumble of her red-gold hair that framed the smooth face, and her slender neck … he checked himself quickly as he became aware of the new strange feelings he was experiencing towards his travelling companion, and at the same moment he realised that her clear hazel eyes were open and amusedly studying *him*. She smiled, and rolling away from him onto her side, asked, 'Could you please put some suntan lotion on my back?'

Feeling rather embarrassed at the fact that Nathalie had actually caught him staring at her, admiring her in fact, and hoping fervently that she was not a mind reader, Perry only too willingly poured a generous amount of liquid into his hands and began to apply it to Nathalie's warm skin. As he massaged the lotion into the back of her neck and shoulders, he felt an unaccustomed reaction to the sensuality of the contact between his hands and the smoothness of her silky skin. His fingers suddenly felt hot, as if from an electric shock, and very, very sensitive!

After he'd finished the task, he quickly turned away from Nathalie, afraid that she'd notice the hard swelling inside his swimming trunks, that were also quite skimpy. *'I've not felt like this for a long time! I must remember that she is only my travelling companion and still grieving for her dead husband, and not anything more. What am I? A gawping teenager? I have to get a grip of my emotions!'*

Just as he'd finished admonishing himself, Nathalie leaned across him. As she did so, he inhaled a scent of fragrant shampoo, suntan lotion, and an almost indefinable odour of warmth and – woman.

'Would you like some lotion on *your* back, Perry? This sun is very strong and you don't want to burn.'

'Oh, yes please!' He was stammering like a stupid schoolboy, and after rolling onto his front he turned his hot face into the towel, away from his companion's observant eyes. Then he felt a gentle touch as Nathalie in turn smoothed the lotion onto his back, across his neck and wide shoulders, then down, down to the small of his back. He wondered if it was his wishful imagination, or did her fingers linger just a bit? The pressure of his hard-on had by then become so unbearable that he suddenly found it very necessary to turn away from her, jump to his feet, mumble something incomprehensible and walk away across the sand, knowing he had left his companion somewhat puzzled.

* * *

Later the same night, lying in the darkness and privacy of the narrow bed in his vehicle, he chastised himself for allowing his feelings to assert themselves. After all, he hadn't really known her long enough to reach the stage of … His thoughts churned round and round in his head, and he realised that he held Nathalie in very high esteem, which was far more than just sexual attraction. Apart from all her obvious physical attributes, he admired the courage she'd shown after losing her entire family so tragically; he respected her outlook on all the important aspects of life; he enjoyed her gentle, whimsical sense of humour; he just enjoyed spending time with her!

His imagination visualised her lying close to him in her rather larger tent. Did she sleep on her side, curled up like a little kitten, or did she spread herself on her back, her tangled bright hair framing her face, her arms opened wide? Did she wear pyjamas, or perhaps a pretty little nightie – or was she naked …?

'This had got to stop!' he told himself firmly. 'She is a good friend and we are sharing an adventure together – possibly exposing ourselves to danger. Who knows? But don't even *begin* to examine just how much you like – fancy – this brave, beautiful woman!' Having reached this sensible decision, he drifted into a restless sleep plagued with lustfully erotic, fantasy dreams, which he carefully blanked from his mind the next morning.

* * *

The next day they began to plan their route to the town of Sparta and the ancient ruins of Mystras. They would follow the scenic coast road past Pyrgos and cross inland to Kalamata on the south coast. From there it was just a short mountain-crossing to their final destination.

As they leant over the map, Perry couldn't help noticing the vulnerable curve of his companion's slender neck. She'd tied her hair into a ponytail, but escaping strands curled into the nape of her neck. He suddenly realised just how very happy he was that she'd decided to join him on this adventure, and admired her resolution to expose the actions, if it were possible, of her beloved grandfather, even if it became obvious that he'd been guilty of committing some sort of crime.

When they had previously talked about this aspect of their search, Nathalie had said, 'Well, it appeared that my grandfather didn't carry out the retrieval of whatever he hid, and was content to live his life without the benefits, or otherwise. After my grandmother died, he certainly never told me that he'd any wish to visit Greece.' Then she cried in some distress, 'Why did my grandfather need to leave his homeland like a refugee? Did he really commit a crime? Or had something come into his possession by accident that had made him so afraid of staying in Germany that he'd made a new home, and taken a new name in another country? It's all too late to ask him now! If he *had* committed a crime, maybe he'd regretted whatever he'd done and was keen for the secret to die with him ... he still *kept* the map though ... didn't he?'

Much as Perry would have liked to put Nathalie's mind at ease, there was not much he could add except to comment mildly, 'Maybe he'd forgotten the map even existed until his whereabouts were discovered, and it's clear that, as he didn't destroy it, he definitely wanted you to own it! Perhaps he even hoped you *would* carry out his quest for him!'

Nathalie derived some comfort from this suggestion and wondered if her grandfather was perhaps watching her present actions with approval.

On the campsite the next evening, sitting outside their diverse sleeping areas in the cool darkening air, eating fresh bread, salad and chicken accompanied by a crisp white wine, Nathalie began hesitantly to ask Perry about his family.

Rather sadly he confessed to her his reluctance to leave his children and how he'd had no option but to make a life without them because his wife had wanted to live with another man.

'I hope you don't mind me asking,' Nathalie said tentatively after a short pause, 'but even after all this, do you still love your ex-wife?'

'Oh, no! She killed our relationship stone dead years ago, as far as I'm concerned. Nowadays, she's just the mother of my two boys. It's them I miss – and now I feel we're growing apart. Each year that passes I'm becoming more of a stranger to them. Their lives are busy and I'm not part of their routine anymore.'

Perry felt a touch of moisture in his eyes as he talked about Tom and Alex, and suddenly felt Nathalie's hand closing softly over his bare arm. 'You must have been a great father. It's clear you loved your boys very much. But you are still young and perhaps you will be a father again, and, next time, will choose a woman who *really* loves you and is *eager* to share your life!' She ended the last sentence quite forcefully, sounding almost angry.

As Perry, surprised by this suggestion, and the vehemence of its delivery, stared curiously at Nathalie, she suddenly blushed and jumped to her feet. 'I'll wash the plates, it's getting late,' she muttered as she gathered up the cutlery and crockery.

Watching her depart to the campsite sinks, Perry stayed seated in the comforting darkness and felt a glow of hope growing within him. Was Nathalie … growing fond of him? Could she be moving on in her own life, in her emotions? Then he shook his head. No, it was too much to hope for. She was just being her normal kind self, encouraging him to look forward to a brighter future.

For her part, as she busily washed up at the communal sink, she wondered if she'd overstepped the mark by the way she'd spoken to Perry. She was puzzled by her own reaction to the way Perry's ex-wife had treated him. The bald facts he'd told her had touched a nerve and caused her to feel very angry. She could still see Perry's surprised blue eyes staring at her searchingly, and her cheeks still felt hot with embarrassment at her reaction. But Perry hadn't deserved to be abused in such a way. He was such a lovely, kind, respectful, thoughtful man. She tried to ignore the fact that he was also very attractive and how much she enjoyed being close to him. He made her feel very safe and protected, and rather special. Then she reluctantly decided that he was probably always like that with the people in his life. He was just a very pleasant person and she was lucky to be sharing this adventure with him.

She recalled her first introduction to this good-looking man, when she'd answered her front door to find him standing firmly on her doorstep. Right from that first moment she'd felt a connection, an empathy, and known that she could respect and trust him. His solid frame and vivid blue eyes radiated a straightforward honesty, and from the moment he'd first gazed at her she'd known that she would be safe and well cared for while she was in his company. Well, now they had developed a valuable friendship and the last thing she wanted to do was spoil their time together by bringing emotions into it.

That night, while Perry was lying in bed, he recalled Nathalie's surprising reaction to the woeful tale of his marriage break-up. She had sounded quite angry about the way Pamela had treated him. What had Nathalie said? *'Next time when you find someone who really loves you'?* In his mind he tested the veracity of that comment along with the implication that he'd not met that person yet. Now, for the first time since his marriage break-up, he wondered if Pamela *had* ever truly loved him.

Always a light-hearted, flip sort of person, she'd never been the type to declare any serious emotions. So why had she been attracted to him?

Trying hard to analyse the way his ex-partner's mind had worked, an uncomfortable thought occurred to him. Was it all because he'd been able to buy her a house? After all it was unusual at his age. He'd been lucky enough to inherit a sizeable sum of money while in his mid-twenties which had enabled them to buy a home outright. Let's face it, he thought bluntly, he'd been so totally, passionately, perhaps blindly in love with Pamela then, he was only too eager to please her. The house had been her choice, of course, although he had agreed to the purchase, and it had proved to be a pleasant home to live in, especially with no mortgage to pay each month. He recalled how much Pamela had hated living in the council flat she shared with her dissatisfied mother and bullying, overbearing stepfather, before they became a couple. Had she hated it sufficiently to see him as a means of escaping the unpleasant conditions she had been living in? They were certainly living in some style, so perhaps she was 'cocking a snook' at her obnoxious stepfather?

With all these worrying thoughts nagging at him, sleep became elusive. He remembered overhearing a conversation between Pamela and some of her friends. She had been bragging about the house in such a manner that Perry had felt embarrassed on her behalf. She had also been crowing about how handsome her two sons were compared to a – thankfully – absent friend, and noting how ugly their daughter was.

'I knew that Perry would father good-looking children,' she'd claimed. 'That's one of the reasons I picked him!'

Perry remembered feeling amused by that statement at the time, but now he wondered if that had been a serious factor – plus the money of course – in attracting her to 'fall in love' with him. In the early days they'd enjoyed an ecstatically satisfying sex life, but it had tailed off to the occasional event after the children were born. Believing Pamela to be too tired, he'd jibbed at putting even more pressure on her when he knew how tiring two small toddlers could be to look after.

If it was the case that Pamela had never truly loved him at all, she must have finally become sufficiently bored to trawl around until she'd found someone else who excited her more than he'd ever done. If so, she'd achieved her aim when she began an affair with Roger, a neighbour living a few streets away Financially she had done well too because, for the children's sake, he'd agreed to give her the rights to the house in their divorce settlement.

Who knows? he thought, perhaps she was just as bored with his replacement by now. Suddenly he was pleased to note that he truthfully didn't care in the slightest about her.

Just before he finally drifted off to sleep, his concluding thought was that Nathalie had probably been right in her assessment; he had not yet found a woman who truly loved him. If only he'd been lucky enough to find someone like Nathalie who, when she eventually found *her* man, would love him deeply and completely, without limits, as she must have truly loved Bernard before he was so tragically killed.

* * *

The next day they reached the large town of Kalamata and parked on the quayside with the intention of doing some shopping and afterwards finding a pleasant taverna for lunch. They'd encountered some difficulty in finding somewhere to park as the area was very busy, but eventually they managed to find a narrow space on a quayside car-park into which Perry skilfully edged the Safari. The likelihood of any discomfort lingering between them after Nathalie's impulsive outburst seemed to have dispersed during the night and they were both glad to revert to their former uncomplicated friendliness.

As Nathalie carefully opened the passenger door and slipped nimbly to the ground, she said jokingly, 'I'll need to make sure I don't scratch or dent this beauty next to us, getting in or out!' She was referring to a sleek, shiny black sports car parked next to their vehicle.

Perry smiled wryly as he viewed the car. 'It's a Lamborghini,' he said. 'I don't think my insurance would cover even the tiniest scratch.'

They wandered along the quayside looking at the few shops that lined the seafront, and were soon glad to turn inland, away from the heat. After a short walk they found themselves in one of the more shaded shopping areas. Now early May, the weather was becoming much hotter, and it was pleasant to slow down and take things easy in the welcome coolness of the street, it being shaded by tall buildings and a line of trees.

* * *

It was more than three hours before they returned to the vehicle. They'd wandered far towards the centre of Kalamata before they had decided to eat in the cool dappled garden of a taverna. A Greek meal was always a slow and lengthy experience, but all the more enjoyable for that.

As they neared the seafront, they could see flashing lights, an ambulance, a fire engine and crowds of people on the edge of the quay in the area where Perry's van had been parked. Something had happened during their absence! Was their vehicle damaged? As they reached the edge of the crowd of onlookers they could see that right next to where their own vehicle was parked, the low wall along the edge of the quay had been demolished.

'That was where the Lamborghini was parked,' cried Perry. 'Whatever has happened?'

The press was in evidence, taking pictures of the broken wall and the quayside, and craning over to take shots of the water below. A worried Perry questioned a number of the onlookers and eventually discovered that the Lamborghini belonged to a well-known Greek pop star, Yannis Karatasos, and that he'd reversed the car through the wall and into the water below. It was thought that he had done it intentionally, hence the additional media interest. In the water below the quay, the rescuers were in the process of extracting the driver from his submerged car, while the paramedics were standing by for emergency treatment as the shout had gone up that he was still alive.

Observing the media personnel with dismay, Perry quickly pulled Nathalie away from the scene. 'Our vehicle will be in all the Greek newspapers, probably on television, and God knows where else now! It's part of the background scene of this tragedy. We just have to hope that our pursuers, if there still are any, aren't in Greece yet, and if they are that they don't recognise the vehicle. We mustn't be seen to be associated with it in any way, and let's make sure our faces aren't in any of the photographs!'

As soon as the press had departed and most sightseers had quit the scene, the couple, their faces shrouded by large hats, jumped hurriedly into their vehicle and decided to find an interim campsite just outside Kalamata rather than continue on to Sparta: a safeguard just in case they'd already been identified. The last thing Perry wanted to do was lead their enemies right to their target. Hopefully, it would have been much too early for anyone to be able to reach the area so quickly; even so, they still kept an eye out in case anyone attempted to tail them. But the roads were very quiet in the late afternoon.

'We'll stay here for a few days and then make a quick dash for a campsite near Sparta. We're crossing the mountains on a minor route anyway, so it's not likely that anyone will see us. There's really only the remotest chance that someone will have spotted the Safari in any of the media reports. And if they have, they're bound to be watching the main road.' Perry spoke encouragingly, as much for himself as for Nathalie. He hoped desperately that the incident in Kalamata hadn't jeopardised their quest just as it had got underway.

As an extra precaution, he'd found a good hiding place for the map inside the tubing which formed the bicycle rack. First he placed the map inside a black plastic bag to protect it from any damp and to render it almost invisible inside its hiding place. After inserting the map, he made sure that the tubing seal was firmly back in place.

The next day they were able to cadge a lift into Kalamata from a friendly Swedish neighbour camping close by. Once in the town, their first objective was to purchase a newspaper, and when they saw the front page they both gasped with dismay. A large front-page picture of the accident scene included the sinking car, the quay crammed with rescue service vehicles, personnel and equipment, the shattered wall of the quayside, the media, and, to the side of the picture in pride of place and only partly obscured by all the activity, their American Safari van.

As neither Perry nor Nathalie could understand Greek, they finally managed to accost an English-speaking passer-by, who kindly read the story to them. In a small patch of shade they found a low stone wall to sit on as they absorbed the impact of the newspaper report. It appeared that the pop star owner of the Lamborghini had been recently dumped by his latest lover, and it was strongly suspected to have been no accident that the car had slammed through the harbour wall. The media and friends of the celebrity believed it had been a suicide attempt – or at least a means to shock his ex-lover into undergoing a change of heart about leaving him.

Although Yannis Karatasos was still alive, he was presently lying in hospital in a deep coma accompanied by a number of broken bones.

'God knows what the *television* coverage was like, but it's probable that our vehicle would have been well in view to anyone watching,' commented Perry wryly. 'Still, we must remember that it doesn't resemble the vehicle those people were looking for – it's a different colour, has a different registration number and is festooned with accessories!'

Their most important quest in the large busy town was to purchase a couple of bicycles. Perry had decided that this would be a good move, especially as he'd already installed the rack on the vehicle, and it would look more authentic if it actually carried what it was intended for. Best of all, they would be able to use the bicycles for their journey back to the campsite. Eventually, they managed to haggle their way to a good deal on a couple of sturdy mountain bikes, obtaining a discount for purchasing two at the same time.

'Now, all we have to do is ride back to the camp!' Perry exclaimed triumphantly. Noticing the dismayed expression on Nathalie's face he queried, 'What's up?'

'Nothing at all!' Nathalie grimaced. 'It's just that I haven't ridden a bike since I was a child. I'll probably fall off.'

Perry smiled encouragingly. 'You'll be fine! It's something you never forget how to do. Just follow me and shout if you have a problem.'

More than an hour later they arrived back at the campsite, hot and ready to cool off in the swimming pool. But first, the bikes were carefully lashed onto the frame. Nathalie had managed the journey without any mishaps, although she'd wobbled about a bit at first until she'd got the hang of steering again. Once she'd regained her confidence, she had had to admit that the experience had been very pleasurable, even though her rear end felt more than a little bruised by the unaccustomed hard saddle.

Lying refreshed at the edge of the pool, Perry glanced at Nathalie, now relaxed once more, her skin turning from a soft pink to an attractive gold. He said thoughtfully, 'All we need to do now is make a run for the campsite we've chosen near Sparta and hide ourselves in it until we've achieved our visit to Mystras.'

'You're sure it will be safe for us to move?' groaned Nathalie, wishing they could stay a little longer. The pool was so inviting, and it was all too easy to forget they were only together to complete a mission rather than enjoy a wonderful holiday as a couple of close friends. After all, without the existence of the map, she'd never even have met Perry, let alone be spending a great holiday with him. *No,* she chastised herself firmly, *this man is only here because he found a map that was meant for me. It's more of a business trip really.* Despite her best intentions to keep control of her feelings, her heart sank as she absorbed this undeniable truth.

'The sooner we settle into the Sparta site the better,' Perry assured her. 'Perhaps we'll be able to find a pitch that's more obscured from view – just in case – although we're probably safe enough anyway. Let's have a swim while the sun's still so hot, shall we?'

Soon they were splashing and frolicking happily in the refreshingly chill water, only too glad to forget for a while the challenge ahead of them.

FIVE

Leaning back comfortably in his old, folding canvas chair, Perry sighed with pleasure. The campsite near the town of Sparta was fairly busy and large enough for their purposes, the groves of olive trees providing plenty of shade and, more importantly, plenty of cover. Parked beneath them and between a couple of bushes, to anyone glancing around casually the Safari was almost totally invisible in the darkness behind the enveloping screen of the dense greenery. They'd also placed Nathalie's tent in front of the hidden van to obscure the view even further. For the time being they would not of course be able to use the vehicle, but they had already hired a small, inconspicuous car from a company in Sparta to use for longer journeys, and they had the bikes for shorter distances.

As Perry watched Nathalie folding away some freshly washed clothes in the shade of her roomy tent, he cast his mind back to their recent journey. He was convinced they had not been spotted, or followed to the site. They had gathered as many provisions as possible before leaving the Kalamata campsite and had turned onto the much shorter but mountainous route to Sparta. Although the road was fairly well surfaced, the gradients were steep and in places the route had become perilously narrow. The main benefit had been that traffic on the road was sparse, with most cars opting for the longer but faster route along the coast to Githio, and only then turning inland to Sparta and onwards towards Tripoli. The scenery had been absolutely wonderful with the green hills below them gradually fading to mauve in the distance until they merged with the incredible deep blue of the sea.

He sighed. It was hard to believe that now they were only a stone's throw from their target, the ancient ruins of Mystras. Now all they had to do was pick a day, and a time, and then see if they could unravel the sketchy instructions that had been reduced to symbols on the tattered old map, and find whatever Nathalie's grandfather had seen fit to hide away all those years ago. However, Perry was finding it only too easy to be seduced by the lovely warmth of the weather, the beautiful surroundings, and of course the tantalising presence of his companion. It seemed almost a crime to waste the enjoyment of the holiday, and only too easy to forget about possible threats to their safety.

After spending so much time together, he and Nathalie knew a lot about each other's history. Their conversation flowed easily and they had each learned to value the opinion of their travelling companion. Perry had learnt that Nathalie and her husband had been together since children and, as good loyal friends, had drifted into a marriage that had proved a safe, steady, reliable environment for them to enjoy. But Perry began to wonder if, after all, Nathalie had ever really known the power, excitement and wonder of a magnetic sexual attraction. Had she really been in love with Bernard?

Then he wondered about his own previous love life. What if he asked himself the same question? He believed he'd loved his wife when they were first married, and in the early days too until her coldness towards him had eventually, and unmistakeably, indicated that someone else had become the object of her affection. The very new feelings he was now experiencing towards Nathalie he never remembered feeling when he'd been with his ex-wife, not at any time. Was Nathalie also experiencing similar new sensations? Sometimes when she looked at him, Perry felt that her eyes had a startled expression as if she was not sure what she was feeling anymore, and was not fully in control of her emotions. For his part, as well as an almost unbearable sexual attraction, he felt a tenderness towards her that he'd never experienced before and an overpowering urge to care for her, to protect her from unpleasantness. He acknowledged to himself that, even if it could prove problematic for them both, if she were to give him any indication, make any move towards him, he would find it extremely difficult, if not entirely impossible, to resist her

How easily the time slipped past! He was savouring every moment they spent together; the surroundings were lovely, the temperature was seductively warm, and Nathalie seemed to be enjoying his company as much as he craved being close to her. Even when they were just performing the most mundane of tasks, every job had become fun because they were sharing the work. He knew Nathalie was enjoying herself – she was actually laughing these days, even at some of his corny jokes – and he could only hope that she too might be feeling there was something significant growing between them.

Only yesterday evening, an incident had occurred that was quite comical, leastways to him, and Perry had realised just how easy it would be to forget any common sense. He had begun to prepare for bed in the van after Nathalie had zipped herself into her tent, when suddenly he'd heard her scream – well, less of a scream, more of a muffled squawk.

Quickly jumping out of the van, he'd found Nathalie, half-dressed, outside her tent looking very distressed.

'What's up?' Perry had asked anxiously.

'There is a moth in my tent! It is a huge one!'

Trying hard to smother a smile, Perry had said, 'Well, I suppose you'd like me to remove it for you?'

'Oui! Oh, yes! I would be very grateful, Perry, if you would!'

Perry smiled again. He loved the way Nathalie used her natural language in a crisis. They had both flapped towels at the pesky insect, which proved very stubborn as well as elusive. Eventually, after a lot of encouragement, the moth fluttered out, leaving the two occupants very hot, breathless and exhausted. By that time they were both laughing uncontrollably at their own antics, and had collapsed onto the ground in a tangled heap.

'I don't know why I get so freaked by insects! I could have done that myself without bothering you,' Nathalie had at last gasped.

'What! And do me out of this hilarity?' Perry grinned as he gazed into her eyes. Suddenly he'd been aware of the intimacy of their closeness – their bodies touching and arms clasping each other, and felt a heat rising within him. The dreamy expression in Nathalie's golden eyes and her sudden intake of breath had raised his hopes that she'd felt similarly. However, he had not wanted to spoil the moment by taking advantage of the situation, so he'd kissed her lightly on the nose and then gently pulled himself free from her embrace.

Clambering to his feet, and trying hard to control his breathlessness and speak in a normal voice, he'd said, 'You should be fine now. Have a good night's sleep, but always call me if you have a problem. I'm at your service, ma'am!' He had given her a mock salute and quickly exited her tent.

Although he was serious about being watchful and not complicating his and Nathalie's relationship, sometimes he wondered if they were being ridiculous, paranoid, about someone wanting to follow them all the way to Greece. Then he reminded himself what had already happened to Nathalie's family, and how he'd been trailed from Manchester to his home. If only they could forget about any danger and threats to their safety, how wonderful this trip could be! Sighing, he rationalised that without this quest in the first place, Nathalie wouldn't have been keeping him company at all.

He loved that she was so caring and sympathetic. Earlier, when he'd been watching a group of young children in the campsite playing together – French, Dutch, English, Italian – different languages never seemed to bother small children, they always seemed to manage and play well together – although he'd been smiling at their antics, his heart was heavy because these days he never saw his boys playing together anymore, and he missed them like crazy. As he stood there, he'd felt a gentle hand on his shoulder. Nathalie had been reading his mind and knew he was feeling sad. Instantly he'd felt a warm feeling of comfort.

After a silence, she'd said slowly, 'I always wonder what my child would have been like. I knew it would have been a girl and would have now been about as old as that child over there.' She pointed to a dainty little elf of a girl who was dancing around energetically.

Perry had turned and clasped Nathalie's hand; it had been his turn to offer comfort. 'I'm being selfish indulging myself in misery about my boys, who are both alive and well, while you actually lost your child and have truly nothing left but grief. I'm so sorry for your heart-breaking experience, Nathalie.'

In a mutual offering of sympathy, they'd clasped each other in a warm embrace for a few golden moments, until feelings of embarrassment had driven them apart.

**

A day later, when they were spending the evening with English neighbours, sitting outside the pleasant, middle-aged couple's tent, sharing a couple of bottles of wine, and enjoying a chat about their respective holidays, their host, Ken, leant back in his chair, took a good sip from his glass – and dropped a bombshell.

'We did a day trip to Kalamata yesterday and a funny thing happened, didn't it, Laurie? We were stopped by a group of Germans – well, they sounded German, just as we were about to get into our car. They weren't tourists by their appearance and they asked us a lot of questions. Were we staying in a hotel or were we camping? Had we seen an Englishman driving an American camper van on any sites we'd been on – or anywhere for that matter? Bit weird! They showed us a newspaper picture of a vehicle. Perhaps somebody's committed a crime or something …' Their neighbour tailed off.

His wife pulled a face and said, 'We didn't like their attitude at all. A couple of the men were older and they were very curt with us. Made us feel we'd got to give them an answer. I almost felt as if I'd done something wrong and had been pulled into a police station for interrogation!' She laughed at her own comment.

Both Nathalie and Perry smiled nervously. 'How very odd! What did you tell them?' Perry asked, his heart pumping rapidly, hoping that his camper van was sufficiently hidden and hadn't been recognised by anyone as the American vehicle in question – especially now that someone was definitely searching for them.

Ken answered. 'Oh, we told them we'd not seen any American vans. We haven't, but even if we had, we wouldn't have told them, because of their unpleasant attitude. I'm sure they were not just looking out for a friend, judging by the expression on their faces! Anyway, as we said to them, who'd want to travel long distances in American vehicles. Everybody knows they cost an arm and a leg – and loads of Euros to feed them with fuel! They're all gas-guzzlers!' Their neighbour laughed loudly at the very thought.

Nathalie glanced at Perry as they both breathed a sigh of relief. Perry was glad he'd not boasted about the cheaper cost of travelling around due to the Safari's LPG gas conversion. Although there were probably no fuelling opportunities in Greece, and few in other countries, it cost him a lot less to fill up when he did find the facilities. For the rest of the time he was able to run on petrol anyway. He thanked the good fortune that a previous owner had seen fit to install the system. Perhaps it had been Nathalie's grandfather?

However, what *was* obvious to both of them now was that the vehicle had been sufficiently identified via the newspaper or television pictures to draw their pursuers to check out the possibility of the Safari pictured being the exact vehicle they were searching for, even if they weren't entirely sure. It also indicated that they'd followed the instructions on Perry's fake map and had drawn the obvious blank. Or perhaps they'd always realised that the map was a fake, once they'd had time to examine it closely.

'Very strange indeed,' murmured Perry, noncommittally.

Inside his body he felt his blood run cold as he realised how close their pursuers were. He would need to devise a plan to put into effect if their whereabouts were discovered. Although he hated the idea, Nathalie would need to disassociate herself from him and keep herself safe, especially as these people didn't seem to know anything about her. With her separate tent and the hire car, there was no reason for anyone who located him to connect Nathalie with his quest at all.

Then another thought occurred to him. What if, when they visited Mystras, they were successful with their search? If that were the situation and their pursuers then caught up with them, they'd immediately gain possession of whatever he and Nathalie had found. Perry decided to put pen to paper once he was back in the van. It would be just as well to have something – an emergency arrangement to fall back on – if the worst-case scenario actually happened.

Once back outside Nathalie's tent, Perry whispered, 'We've got to go to Mystras tomorrow. Our time is running out. Someone will identify us to these Germans eventually if they ask enough people. They've only got to start making their enquiries in different campsites and they'll find us. The campsite owner will not have any compunction about telling them what they want to know. I'm surprised Ken hasn't already poked around in the bushes and identified my vehicle, and if he does, he's bound to realise it's exactly the type that those people were looking for!'

He mused for a moment and added, 'However, there's one good thing we've learnt – they really don't know anything at all about you. They're only looking for a solo traveller – me! We've got to find whatever your grandfather hid, then if we believe it really was something he'd stolen during the war, try if possible to return it to the original owners – or the correct authority – and get out of the country quickly. Do you agree with this, Nathalie? The bit about returning the find to the rightful owner?'

'Oh yes!' Nathalie exclaimed. 'Whatever it is, it has been responsible for two deaths already. It will be like lifting a curse and ending the whole debacle.' She stared straight into Perry's eyes and murmured, 'Perhaps then, we can just be two people, a normal couple enjoying an unforgettable holiday.'

As she glanced away, Perry noticed the slight flush on her cheeks and wondered if she really had intended to imbue the sentence with such meaning. She was now obviously embarrassed by her statement, but as Perry had looked at her slightly parted lips and the lovely golden dreamy quality of her eyes as she'd gazed so intently at him a moment ago, he was immediately reminded of the almost uncontrollable emotions he'd felt when they'd been so close together the other night. His heart flipped over a few times in response to her suggestion and was still pumping hard. He hoped Nathalie hadn't noticed how breathless he'd suddenly become. Now he needed to reply, and to choose his words very carefully.

'That is a great idea, something to really look forward to,' he said quietly.

Nathalie glanced uncertainly at him and then quickly jumped to her feet. 'Time for a coffee, I think!' she cried, disappearing into the depths of her tent.

Later, in the darkness of his van, Perry reflected on the fact that he could listen forever to the wonderfully attractive lilt of Nathalie's voice. Although she had a perfect grasp of the English language, there would always be that different, tell-tale pronunciation – she'd never lose that. Plus her endearing, occasional lapse into her own tongue, especially whenever she became stressed or upset. Then he smiled. Who was he kidding? He loved everything about her: walking with her, talking to her, eating with her, swimming, sunbathing, washing up, cleaning – every minute he spent with her was fun and a time to treasure. All in all, he never wanted their time together to end – never!

SIX

The anxious couple made an early start the next day, intent on visiting the ruined Byzantium city of Mystras, now a UNESCO World Heritage site, before too many tourists had time to arrive. After following the signs, they arrived at the end of the rugged access road and parked their inconspicuous rental car among the scattering of saloon cars, rugged four-by-fours and motor caravans. There were no tourist coaches yet as they walked slowly in the rapidly increasing heat towards the ticket entrance to the old city.

Once they were through the entrance building, Nathalie's glance encompassed the various footpaths that led off in different directions before eventually disappearing between shrubs and a variety of ancient, stone-built structures.

'Which way do we go? Does the map indicate anything?' She looked perplexed at the number of possibilities.

Perry studied the folded leaflet he'd just acquired from the young man, darkly handsome and friendly, probably a student, who was selling the entrance tickets, and studied the plan of the ancient city.

'I really don't know. I wish I did. We can't even be sure if the entrance is in the same place as it was when your grandfather sneaked in to search for a good hiding place. There certainly wouldn't have been a ticket office in action during the war. We need to find somewhere to sit, out of view and in the shade, so we can compare your grandfather's map with this plan and see if we can work out what direction to take. This place is huge – much bigger than I thought it would be. Looking at the plan, the whole city is spread across the side of this hill, with a castle called the Citadel on the top of the ridge. It would take days to walk around and visit all the buildings on this site.'

Nathalie looked puzzled. 'But I thought you told me you'd been here before, when you were young, with your parents?'

'Oh, no.' Perry looked ashamed. 'I'm afraid the idea of looking around a crumbling old city hadn't appealed to me then. I opted to stay on the campsite and just lounge around.'

Nathalie laughed. 'A normal teenager, then?'

'Erm, well, yes. Ignorant, and probably one of the worst.'

After finding a low wall in a shady corner, they sat and compared the two maps. One was a printed tourist plan that Perry passed over to Nathalie, and the other her grandfather's crumpled, handwritten map with a scrawl of names and symbols.

'This is not going to be an easy task,' Perry concluded slowly, having studied the scribbled map for some moments. 'The good news is that the entrance does seem to be unchanged. Assuming this is so, it appears that we must make our way to the left of the plan. What buildings will this path lead to?'

'The chapel of Saint George and the monastery of Peribleptos,' answered Nathalie, studying the official plan carefully.

'Perhaps this scrawl here indicates Saint George and the dragon,' mused Perry. 'It's not the best of drawings. Your grandfather's talents obviously didn't lie in that direction! However, we've not got any other clue, so we'll try the chapel of Saint George first.'

Following the left-hand path, they were soon inside the pretty little, well-preserved chapel. Standing in the very welcome cool darkness, they waited a few seconds for their eyes to become accustomed to the gloom, and then quickly glanced around the interior.

'Now what?' Nathalie queried.

'Just look for any sign or symbol that seems unusual.'

'At least this place is quite small, but there's nowhere to really hide anything.'

They both studied the old map again and then Nathalie pointed to a small arrow close to the roughly drawn emblem of Saint George.

'Perhaps that means we've got to continue along this path to the next building. What is its name – the Perib …?'

'Peribleptos,' supplied Perry, glancing at the official guide again. 'It's very old – a mid-14th century monastery, and looks to be a much larger building than this little chapel.'

'That must be it.' Nathalie pointed ahead to a structure barely visible through the greenery of the treetops.

The pathway leading to the monastery was dappled with light and shade cast by the overhanging trees. As they walked along, Nathalie glanced through the foliage to the valley, which dropped away steeply far below, and marvelled at the beauty of the rugged, unspoilt scenery before her. She was taken completely unawares when Perry's arm suddenly wrapped itself as tightly as a metal band around her waist, bringing her to an immediate standstill.

Her shocked gaze was drawn to the sight of a huge snake, writhing across the path right in front of them. Even before she'd realised exactly *what* she was looking at, it was already slithering rapidly over the low, crumbling stone wall, and in a second had completely vanished.

'*Merde!*' she exclaimed shakily. 'That must 'ave been more than a metre long. And I nearly walked into it!'

Even Perry's face had lost its healthy tan. 'It was certainly a big one. But it would have been more scared of us than we were of it.'

'You speak for yourself!' Nathalie shot back sarcastically. However, she quickly stretched up and kissed Perry gently on the cheek. 'I thank you for your speedy action,' she said quietly.

'You're welcome,' responded Perry, still feeling the effects of the light butterfly touch of her lips upon his skin and trying to sound as normal as possible.

They quickly, but more watchfully, continued along the path to the monastery and stood outside the ancient building in awe. The curved walls, built of smooth, honey-coloured stone, radiated the warmth absorbed from the sunlight. A pretty red-tiled dome topped the structure, beneath which the tiled surrounds of the arched windows shaped the domed roof into a beautiful curve. Lower arched windows, set into the walls appeared like mysterious dark eyes peering out from the interior.

'Oh, how beautiful it is,' Nathalie whispered.

'It's lovely, and what a setting! It's built into the rock-face, and terraced on the side of this steep hill,' Perry said. He added, 'Look for any of the symbols that are scrawled on your grandfather's map as we enter the monastery. They aren't clear so they could be anything at all.'

'There are some lions above the door, and some flowers,' Nathalie observed as they entered the building.

'They're lilies, I think,' suggested Perry, recalling something he'd read about symbols long ago, and then tensed as, once again, he scanned the map he was holding. 'There's something your grandfather scrawled here that might represent a lily. What do you think?' He indicated the symbol to Nathalie. 'Does this resemble the emblem over the door?'

Nathalie felt a thrill of excitement as she studied the little map. 'Yes, I'm sure it does. It must mean we're in the right place.'

Perry hoped they were as he didn't want to suggest the possibility to Nathalie that there could be lily symbols in most if not all of the other old buildings on the site.

They continued into the cool darkness of the interior, enjoying the refreshing change of temperature from the unremitting heat outside, and waited for a minute to become accustomed to the gloom.

'There are more lily symbols here … and over here too,' exclaimed Nathalie after several minutes. 'How do we know exactly which one to look for?'

'Oh, my God, Nathalie, look! Do you see the wonderful paintings in the dome,' Perry exclaimed, his eyes avidly absorbing the colourful images. And just look at these wall paintings. How fantastic. This one has Jesus riding a donkey into a city – Jerusalem maybe?' After a few more minutes of wandering around, Perry suddenly felt a stab of resentment because he would have loved to spend more time absorbing the fourteenth century frescoes depicting the life of Jesus and the Virgin Mary, such a variety of beautifully preserved images and vibrant, colourful scenes. But it was only momentary, as he reminded himself of why they were there.

'There's no time to look at them now, we've got to keep on searching, Perry. Perhaps we'll come back here another time?' Nathalie suggested hopefully.

'I know, I know,' grumbled Perry. He looked carefully at the old map again and noted a circle surrounded by an arrow drawn partly around it. 'Look at this symbol, Nathalie. See if you can find anything that this could represent. You take this side and I'll look over there,' he suggested.

After about ten minutes of fruitless searching they both admitted defeat.

'I'm sure that angular line next to it, that looks like steps, plus the numbers written underneath must be significant,' Nathalie mused. 'Do you think the small circle indicates this building and the outer, semi-circular arrow means we've got to look *outside*?' she suggested as she leaned across to look at the incomprehensible symbols again.

'You could be right. Surely that stepped line must indicate a staircase. Maybe we've got to look for a set of stairs outside with a lily symbol nearby,' answered Perry. 'Let's see what we can find.' Once again, reluctantly but firmly, he forced his admiration and his eyes away from more of the awesome wall paintings, and the couple walked outside, back through the main entrance door and into the heat and brilliant dazzling light.

Looking around, he observed, 'There's only so far we can go to circle the building. The rear is built into the rock, and the ground just drops away, here, into the valley below.'

There was, however, an outer staircase near the entrance, but after some fruitless searching they had not found a lily symbol anywhere. Because the staircase was close to the main access, a few sightseers were drifting past occasionally and glancing at them.

'Let me see the map again,' Nathalie requested. After a minute, she asked, 'What is this small number here at an oblique angle, and a second number followed by a capital letter L next to it? It's written immediately underneath the stepped line.'

'Let me see. It's a number 6, a number 3 and, yes, it does looks like an L. If your grandfather was English, I'd have said it indicated *Left*.'

Nathalie exclaimed excitedly, 'But it still would. The German word for *left* is *links*.'

'Suppose the first number indicates the number of stones from the ground and the second number, the third stone from the left?' Perry suggested.

Eagerly they counted six uneven layers of stones as best they could, and then counted three stones in from the left side of the staircase.

'It's hard to count a row because the stones are so irregular. Anyway, there's nothing here at all.' A disappointed Nathalie flopped onto the grass.

Perry thought for a moment. 'Wait. Perhaps it's the other way round. We should count three rows from the ground and the sixth stone from the left.'

Although still not yet crowded, a few passing tourists were now looking rather curiously at them as they lingered by the crumbled flight of steps.

They still found nothing at all. Feeling thoroughly dispirited and wondering if their search was a hopeless project after all, they entered the monastery again. Perry made sure to avert his eyes from the paintings this time and they walked through the building towards its southern side. In front of them was another door. This time the door led outside to a ruined part of the structure. The roof of this small area of the building had collapsed completely, but the walls were mostly intact. Facing them was a graceful archway, which they passed through, and saw in front of them another flight of much steeper steps, leading to a small grassy plateau below.

Feeling very excited by the discovery of a second flight, they quickly descended to the lower grassy area. However once at the bottom of the steps, and after a few moments of feverish searching, they were disappointed to realise that there were no more symbols here either. Perry collapsed onto the grass in a small patch of shade cast by the flight of stairs and groaned.

'I don't think we're going to be able to find anything. It would have been different for your grandfather. He only needed the map to spur his memory, but once in the right location he'd have been able to recall exactly where he'd hidden his … objects.'

Stubbornly, Nathalie said, 'We at least need to try the same formula on this flight of stairs. What's the point of giving up now?'

'You're right,' Perry agreed, jumping to his feet. You read out the instructions again and I'll count the rows and stones.'

After checking their results carefully and counting in both directions once more, they again found nothing at all. Hot and dusty, Perry sat down in the shade feeling by now completely dispirited.

'Perhaps, after all, this is not the right place. We may have to try another building and use the formula on other staircases the same as we have here.'

The flatness of his voice betrayed his disappointment, but then he sighed and added, 'Let's at least have a break and something to drink. Maybe our brains will function better afterwards.' He unpacked two bottles of water from his knapsack and passed one to Nathalie. After quenching his thirst, he picked up the map once more and studied the stepped line with the numbers and letter below. Staring at the angular line drawn by Nathalie's grandfather to supposedly depict a staircase, he suddenly had a thought. Hitting his head with his hand, he cried,

'Eureka! I wonder if we're interpreting the numbers wrongly? Perhaps one number indicates a *step* – not a row or a stone.'

They both scrambled to their feet, eager to try this new formula. Identifying the sixth step, they carefully counted the third stone from the left: still nothing.

'Now the third step and the sixth stone from the left,' Perry muttered feverishly. He stood on the third step so that Nathalie could more easily count the irregular-sized stones.

'One, two, three, four, five . . . Oh, my God, Perry! Look! There's a very faint mark scratched onto this stone. It's been weathered and worn away, but I'm sure it's the emblem we're looking for.'

Perry almost fell down the steps in his haste, and by Nathalie's side he carefully grasped the warm stone and felt it budge slightly at his touch. Grasping it firmly he pulled hard. The stone shifted again. He pulled it further towards him until he could just about insert his hand into the cavity behind it. He pulled out a small, dusty weatherproof bag.

'Oh my God, we've found it!' Nathalie danced with excitement. 'My grandfather must have scratched the lily emblem quite deeply into the stone to mark the right spot, otherwise it wouldn't still be visible after all these years.'

Perry stood motionless, quite dazed by their sudden and, by that time, unexpected success. 'Yes, we've finally found it!' he managed at last. 'What we've got to do now is distance ourselves from this place as quickly as possible. We'll get back to the car and then see what's inside the bag. But before we go . . .' He drew an object from his pocket – a small leather pouch. He thrust the pouch behind the stone, which he then pushed firmly back into its original position.

'What are you doing? What was in that bag?' queried Nathalie.

'Oh, just some junk I bought in the market the other day,' Perry replied nonchalantly. 'It's my Plan B. If we're forced to hand over your grandfather's map, it's something for our pursuers to find. Let them work all this out, like we did. Of course, we'll say we drew a complete blank and hope they believe us. That's if they manage to find us.'

'What's your Plan A, then?' asked Nathalie curiously.

'Oh, I'll tell you about that if the situation arises,' promised Perry. 'I'm hoping it won't be necessary to put either plan into action.'

Once back in their small car, its interior baking hot after standing in the sun for so long – he undid the bag and tipped the contents onto Nathalie's lap. A handful of jewels, set into necklaces, earrings and brooches, blazed in a myriad of colours. Completely outclassing all of them, in brilliance if not in hue, was an enormous, colourless, pear-shaped diamond. The sunlight that streamed into the car struck its many facets as they turned it in their fingers and almost blinded them with its radiance.

'Well, what have we here?' mused Perry. 'This looks to be something more important than a mislaid necklace. We'll need to check this out on the Internet and find out if there's any information on this beauty. I wonder if there's anything so up to date as an Internet café in the locality.'

* * *

Sitting in a private corner in a small Internet café they'd found in the town of Sparta after a lot of searching and enquiring, Perry scoured the computer for information on diamonds. They'd been very thirsty after their search, which had taken a lot longer than they'd expected, and had decided it would be safer to visit the town first before returning to the campsite. Now, with cold drinks and sandwiches in front of them, they were keen to reach the appropriate pages on the frustratingly slow operating system of the computer.

'Hurry up, Perry. I can't wait much longer to see what we've found,' Nathalie complained nervously.

'Wait. It's coming up. Oh, there's a whole list of famous diamonds here. It'll take ages going through it all,' groaned Perry.

Leaning across to view the computer screen, Nathalie cried, 'I don't think it will. Look at the entry near the beginning of the list – see, the Akbar Shah Diamond. Read the information. It says it's "pear-shaped, colourless, and weighs 71.70 carats".'

Perry interrupted, '... and nobody knows where it is. It's disappeared. This *must* be the one we've found.' Reading on, he gasped. 'This diamond was reportedly part of the Peacock Throne. Even *I've* heard of that. As I recall, the whole throne was lost.'

Quickly glancing round at the other customers in the café, he hastily moderated his voice. 'We can't let anyone else overhear our conversation and know what we've got.'

He carefully copied down all the salient facts about the diamond, and passed the information to Nathalie. 'I want you to keep this – and the jewels – in your bag.' He pulled the dusty old bag from his pocket and gave it to her. 'The people who are after this don't know anything about you, so it's safer if you carry it.'

As Nathalie tucked the precious pouch safely into her bag, Perry began punching more letters on the computer keyboard.

'What are you looking for now?'

'I'm just finding out who owned this – item – and when it disappeared,' Perry explained. 'Hold on, this looks promising.'

He quickly scanned the information before him and passed on the relevant details to Nathalie. 'Before World War Two, that particular diamond was displayed in the National Archaeological Museum of Athens. Apparently, it is ancient, Persian – from the Mughal Dynasty. (I wondered where the Peacock Throne fitted in.) It was originally much larger, 116 carats. In 1886 it became privately owned and was cut into the smaller, pear-shape size of 71 carats. Acquired by the museum in 1920, along with other artefacts, it had been hidden for safekeeping during World War Two, but somehow the whereabouts of the items had been discovered and looted by the German Army. It has never been recovered and its whereabouts is unknown.'

He put his head in his hands and groaned. 'Oh, my God, what a responsibility, Nathalie. We've actually found an important historical artefact of huge significance.' Glancing at Nathalie, he added, 'I'm so sorry, but it appears that your grandfather *did* steal it, and the other objects. However, I don't think he realised just what he'd gained possession of. No wonder all those people are still in pursuit of him – and now us.'

Shifting his position on the hard plastic chair, he added, 'It's clear that somehow we've got to return this to the National Archaeological Museum in Athens.' He sighed, not wanting to leave the beautiful area they'd been exploring so soon. 'We'd better pack up and set off for Athens just as quick as we can.'

SEVEN

O nce back at the campsite, the couple began packing away their clothes and camping equipment. After an hour or two of steady work, almost all the camping apparatus had been carefully packed into the Safari. By the time they'd finished it was late afternoon, so they decided to enjoy the rest of the day and make a really early start the next morning. It meant they would have to dismantle Nathalie's tent at the last minute because she would still need to use the sleeping area that night, but they considered they could do it very quickly before they set off. After some deliberation they decided that as they still had a couple of days in hand on the rental car, once they were on their way, they would call the company and tell them to pick up the car from the campsite. The rental had already been paid and they would explain that they'd had an unexpected emergency.

They were both sitting in their canvas chairs, chatting quietly and enjoying a cold shandy, which they considered they'd earned after the strenuous efforts involved in collecting, sorting, and packing their belongings so speedily, when their neighbours, Laurie and Ken, drove slowly past them and parked outside their own tent. Laurie, clutching a shopping bag, unzipped the tent and disappeared inside, but after Ken had laboriously clambered from his car, he walked back towards them looking puzzled.

'Hello, you two,' he said. 'I can see you're ready for an imminent departure, but I just wanted to tell you something. A very odd thing. Do you remember I told you about some Germans who questioned us in Kalamata the other day? You do? Well, we've just seen one of them. Laurie recognised him – never forgets a face. Yes, well he was standing outside the office, presumably looking for the site owner.' He laughed sarcastically. 'I don't think he's looking to camp here, anyway. Just not the type.' Noticing the stunned expressions on his neighbours' faces he queried anxiously, 'What is it? You both look ill.' He paused for a moment and then abruptly shot a question at them. 'Do you know who he is – who they are? Looking at the dire expressions on your faces, I believe you do.'

'We need help,' Perry said urgently. 'All we can tell you at this point is that they are bad men and are looking for us. When and if this is resolved, we will tell you everything All I will say is, *we* are trying to do the right thing and return something to the lawful owners.'

Ken smiled grimly. 'So, *you* are the owner of the American motor caravan?' At Perry's nod of affirmation, he added, 'Sorry for some of the comments I made before. I *do* know all about bad people, I'm a newly retired police detective inspector. During my working life I was based in the West Midlands.'

Perry registered that useful fact and then turned to Nathalie.

'*You've* got to leave now, in the rental car. Now!' he told her urgently. He tried to ignore the dismayed expression on her face as he rummaged in his pocket and drew out a folded sheet of paper that he'd had the foresight to prepare earlier.

'Remember I told you I had a plan? This is my Plan A. On here you'll find the name, address, and telephone number of a journalist friend of my family – Antony Bastias. He works in Athens for the *Kathimerini* daily newspaper and he's a good man. As soon as possible after your arrival, phone him and ask him to arrange a meeting between himself, senior staff of the National Archaeological Museum of Athens, and yourself of course. Then you can hand over – well you know what to hand over – with plenty of witnesses to make sure that "you know what" can't disappear again. Then tell Antony to broadcast the event as widely as he can. He'll do this like a shot and naturally make the most of the scoop for his own paper.'

A shocked Nathalie hastily tucked the piece of paper safely into her bag. 'I don't like to leave without you, especially if you'll be in danger,' she said tearfully.

'I'll try and leave, too, very soon, but now they're in the area, they'll probably spot the Safari as soon as it's in the open. If I do manage to get away safely, we'll meet at my friend's home, or the museum, in a day or two. Either way we can keep in contact via our mobiles. Tell Antony everything. He will know what to do about the media and publicity side of things. Once "you know what" has been officially returned, then the sooner our German *friends* find out via the media, the better, as they'll stop looking for us. Tell Antony I need you to stay with him for reasons of safety. He's a good friend, he'll look after you, and you can trust him implicitly.'

Ken cut in anxiously, 'I can see you've got a real problem. I won't ask what "you know what" refers to, but is there anything we can do? At least, come and stand behind my tent so you can't be seen!'

The group moved hastily into the deep shade of Ken's large tent.

Perry said, 'The most important thing is that Nathalie isn't seen with me. Soon these people will have identified me, but they believe I'm travelling solo.'

'Park your rental car outside our tent, then,' urged Ken, and Perry immediately made to rush off to move the vehicle as Ken had suggested. 'No, not you – Nathalie!' hissed Ken. Turning to Nathalie, the ex-policeman in him surfacing readily, he ordered sharply, 'Walk back to the car, out of sight, through the trees, just in case the guy is watching. Park your rental next to our car outside this tent. After you've done that you should walk to our tent as if it were *yours,* and disappear from sight behind it. Return to your tent, next, by the same route, out of sight, and collect your possessions. Bring them back here through the bushes and carefully creep out from behind the tent. When you appear, it will look as if you've gathered your gear from *inside* our tent. You can then load everything into the car outside, here, without attracting any interest. All of this is a precaution, just in case the guy is in the area. It's a remote possibility really, but it's best to be careful. Make sure you've left nothing of yours in Perry's van, otherwise these people will know Perry wasn't alone after all.'

Nathalie grabbed the van keys from Perry and departed stealthily through the trees. The men waited anxiously until they heard the sound of the engine and the car appearing and parking next to Ken's. As a worried-looking Nathalie jumped out and rejoined them, Ken said, 'I'll get Laurie to go to the office and try and distract the guy. If he hasn't found the site owner already, perhaps she can mislead him into believing he won't be back for hours.'

He disappeared into his own tent, leaving the dismayed and distressed couple alone.

'I checked the van. There's nothing of mine left inside,' Nathalie whispered. Then she gulped with emotion. 'But I don't want to leave you, Perry. The idea of you being in danger is awful and I need to stay here in case there's anything I can do to help,' she cried.

Unexpectedly she moved close to Perry, clasped her arms tightly around him and kissed him on the cheek.

'I really care about your safety,' she murmured. 'I really care a lot.'

Perry tightened his arms around her and pulled her even closer against him. His questing mouth fastened onto her soft lips and he heard her sigh. Suddenly, they were both kissing each other hard as if their lives depended on it.

'Ahem.' They were suddenly aware that Ken was back beside them and parted reluctantly, realising that they had more urgent problems to face at the moment.

'Laurie's gone across to delay the fellow if she can, but you'd better get your skates on because she might not be able to stall him for long, if at all.'

Still following Ken's advice, Nathalie crept through the trees back to her tent to collect her possessions, which fortunately were mostly contained in one neat holdall. After returning through the trees by the same route, she tried to appear nonchalant as, seemingly emerging from their neighbours' tent, she carried her holdall and jacket to the rental car and stashed them carefully in the boot.

When she rejoined Perry behind the tent, she cried, 'Why don't you come too? In the rental car. Leave your vehicle here and we can pick it up afterwards.'

'It's too risky,' replied Perry. Sheepishly he said, 'I can't just leave the Safari here – abandon it!' Then he added seriously, 'They've only got to identify me sitting next to you and they'll be after both of us. You leaving on your own is our best chance of returning ...' he glanced at Ken, '... the "you know what" to its owners. Plus, I can play the decoy and ensure you have no problems completing the – task. Maybe I could even stall them if I could get them to believe I've not even been to Mystras yet. I might have to give them the map, though, if that's okay with you?'

Glancing at Nathalie's tearful face as she nodded assent, he said urgently, 'I'll be leaving here in a day or two, just long enough to be sure our followers have moved on. Send me a text once you've arrived, but keep it bland. Don't mention names and places, just in case my mobile falls into the wrong hands. Same goes for any message confirming arrangements to meet. But once the exchange has been made officially to the museum, and the media have been informed, send me a text openly, advising me to watch the national headlines It won't matter if anyone else reads it by then.' He added softly, 'We'll be together again soon, I promise. But now you must go. Are you sure you've got the – "goods" – on you, plus the address? And you *do* know what you have to do?' When she nodded dolefully, he kissed her gently on the cheek and said softly, 'Then go quickly Have courage. Antony will take care of you, my love.'

As Nathalie was driving around the one-way track on her way to the exit, her heart singing at Perry's final term of endearment despite the shadow of danger looming over them, she caught sight of Laurie walking slowly back through the trees towards her tent, using her camera here and there to take some holiday shots, followed at a distance by the site owner and a tall man wearing a dark suit. Although she saw the man glance at the car, he showed no interest once he'd registered there was a woman in the driver's seat, and, although she realised that their plan had worked, she still feared for Perry's safety. But Perry had been right. If he'd been sitting in the car beside her, he would have run the risk of being recognised and their plan would have failed.

As she drove away from the campsite – and Perry – she could still feel the heat of his lips on her own when they'd kissed so passionately, and the wonderful sensations that been aroused between them while their bodies had been so closely welded together. She almost smiled as she wondered whether the rapid thumping of her heart and shortness of breath were due to the stress of the situation they were facing, or the delicious memory of that unexpected embrace

* * *

Hans Stiebling was feeling increasingly frustrated. They'd been so sure that the vehicle pictured on television and in the newspaper at the quayside of Kalamata had been the one they were looking for, but somehow, it had vanished into thin air. It had been cleverly disguised, if indeed it was the one they were searching for. The colour of the paintwork had been changed, accessories added, and it even had a different registration number. However, the important thing had been that it was the right make of vehicle and it was in the right place. As nobody in his team had spotted it leaving the area, the only other explanation had to be that the owner was hiding it from view – perhaps on a campsite?

The proprietor of a campsite on the edge of Kalamata remembered the vehicle but had no idea where the owner was heading, so now he and his team were trying other campsites in the area. It had taken ages to locate this particular site owner, who'd been having a nap and at first was disinclined to answer. Even now he was not being at all helpful. Although he agreed that he might have seen a vehicle similar to the one pictured in the newspaper, he wasn't sure if it was still there. No, he hadn't seen it for a while. As the German never asked about a passenger, the site owner never saw fit to provide information about a woman also being in the vehicle. When Spiros was asked if he could show the German whereabouts the vehicle had been parked, he decided to give his curt questioner the run-around. He just didn't like the man at all – and he'd been woken up too abruptly!

What Hans didn't realise was that many of the wartime-generation Greek residents of the Peloponnese were particularly averse to his race owing to a regrettable incident that had occurred sometime after the end of the Second World War. Spiros' father had told him all about the ill-fated incident, so his son's opinion of Germans was equally low. He didn't anyway like the bossy, overbearing attitude of the tall man in front of him who'd introduced himself as Herr Hans Hausmann, so he was disinclined to tell the man much at all. Greeks are a very loyal, friendly, staunch race but, like elephants, they have long memories.

At this point a middle-aged English lady walked across the campsite towards them, snapping pictures here and there with her small camera. Smiling at them both, she tried to engage them in conversation. Spiros found her behaviour rather puzzling as she seemed to be attempting to delay their walk across the campsite by engaging in small talk; this suited Spiros admirably. However, the German started to lose his temper and insisted that they search the area where the vehicle had last been seen. But even Spiros was not quite sure *exactly* where it had been parked, and considered that perhaps it really *had* gone.

Moving further into the site, Hans watched the older woman walk back towards her tent, still aiming her camera at all and sundry, and felt contemptuous of her asinine conversation. He reflected on the rotten situation that had led him to the necessity of dealing with such stupid people as these two. Idly, through the screen of foliage, he watched a younger woman leave a tent and load something into the boot of her car. She strolled back towards the tent, and then his attention wandered and he looked away as he reflected on previous events. What it boiled down to was, the old man had taken what was theirs. Hans totally ignored the fact that his own family had stolen the items in the first place – that never entered the equation.

It had been insanely bad luck that had led to them losing sight of the vehicle in France, five years ago, just after his father and his comrade had finally located their quarry. They were able, despite the lashing rain, to keep track of the Safari on the autoroute and, just managing to keep it in view once it turned off, had caught sight of the old man as he made his way towards the lights of the service area. They had dragged him towards some outbuildings where they had given him a good beating, but the old man had been defiant and uncooperative and had taunted them by saying the map still existed, but claimed they'd never find it, or the jewels. When he'd finally realised the danger he was in, he gave up in the desperate hope he might live long enough to see his granddaughter once more, and confessed that the map was in the van. They forced him to where he said he'd parked it, only to find that it was gone. Thinking he was still deceiving them, out of fury and frustration they beat him savagely again and threw his lifeless body into the bushes.

Using the papers found on the old man, they were able to locate his home, which they proceeded to ransack in case he had been lying to them. Of course, it yielded nothing, which then left the vehicle as the only possible hiding place for the map, just as the old man had claimed; and it had been stolen from right under their noses. Worse than that, it seemed that it had ended up in Eastern Europe. And now, suddenly, after all these years, the American vehicle had turned up on the Internet; but they'd been too late, it had already been sold to someone in England.

Hans smiled grimly, his blue eyes cold. Obviously, the new owner had found the information by some lucky fluke – and then tried to fool them by faking up a new map. They'd already known from Hans' father that the 'items' were hidden on the Peloponnese, so when the map indicated a hiding place in the ruins of Delphi on the mainland, west of Athens, they'd realised straightaway that it was a fake. Then, of course, after they'd seen the television report about the stupid Greek pop star and his pathetic attempt at suicide, there in centre stage, so to speak, was most probably the vehicle they were searching for! The stupid Englishman obviously didn't know what was at stake, but he'd decided to interfere anyway – to his own cost. Hans smiled darkly. 'Oh, yes' he thought. 'It'll be a case of curiosity killing the cat. Stupid fool.'

The site owner began ambling across the site, and as Hans followed the Greek, he heard a car engine and turned quickly to identify the vehicle. However, it was only the same woman he'd watched before, alone, and he quickly lost interest once more.

Ten minutes' later, Hans realised that the site owner either really didn't know where the Safari had been parked, or he was playing games with him. As he passed the English couple sitting outside their tent, the woman being the same one who had slowed his progress by her irrelevant chatter, he glimpsed a silver and white vehicle parked well out of the way and mostly screened by some large thick bushes. Something about its height made him think that could be it! He took a surreptitious peep. Yes, that could definitely be it all right. However, for the moment, especially as the couple were within earshot, Hans decided to pretend he'd not noticed anything, shook Spiro's hand, thanked him for his time and told him he would obviously have to look elsewhere. He didn't want the Englishman to feel threatened just yet. They'd bide their time, keep him under surveillance – and when the time was right …

But first he needed to confirm it was indeed the right vehicle. After exiting the site, he parked nearby under some trees and waited patiently for nightfall. Then he made his way through the bushes until he reached the rear perimeter of the campsite. Seeing that the boundary fence was strong and in good order, he followed it along until he found what he was looking for – a broken section where someone had obviously taken a short cut back to their unit, probably after a drunken night in town. Sneaking over, he crept like a shadow, deep among the bushes and trees, estimating the whereabouts of his target. Eventually he could just make out the outline of a motor caravan. That was surely it. After observing the vehicle for some moments, he decided that the owner was not inside, or anywhere else close by. Chancing his luck, he silently took a couple of steps and reached the side of the Safari. Taking a coin from his pocket, he carefully scraped at its silver paintwork, revealing, as he had expected, a bright blue colour underneath.

* * *

Perry had been invited to eat with Ken and Laurie Wilding, and sitting in the cool velvety darkness of the evening air outside their tent, they talked over the day's unexpected events.

'The good news is that your vehicle wasn't spotted,' Ken mused. 'We heard the German say he'd be looking elsewhere, so you should be alright holed up here for a while.'

Perry's mobile signalled the arrival of a text.

'I have to read this,' he said apologetically. 'I'm hoping it's from Nathalie at last.'

Thankfully he read the confirmation that Nathalie had arrived safely at Antony's home. He quickly sent a reply asking her to let him know, as briefly as possible of course, when the meeting would be taking place.

'Nathalie had a good journey to Athens and is now safe in the house of my friend,' he informed his companions.

It was then that Perry decided to tell the kindly helpful couple the whole story. He felt that it would be good insurance for somebody of Ken's status as an ex-copper to know the full situation, just in case everything still went pear-shaped. By the time he'd finished telling the whole unhappy story, their food was neglected and mostly uneaten, and both Ken and Laurie were looking at him with shocked eyes.

'So it turns out to be a valuable, no, *priceless* artefact that's been missing for more than fifty years,' gasped Laurie. 'No wonder you were so worried. What a responsibility.' Her large brown eyes were shiny with tears. 'And that poor, poor girl' she exclaimed in distress. 'To lose her grandfather and husband in such a cruel way.'

Ken felt anger consume his body, but his copper's analytical brain was churning over the information. He said thoughtfully, 'These Germans chasing after you must have been, or are connected to, the soldiers in the German army who were stationed in Greece during the war. If they know what Nathalie's grandfather hid, then *they*, as friends or family, must also have been responsible for the original looting of the artefacts. If we only knew their identities, we could report them to the authorities. As it appears that the French never managed to arrest anyone at the time for the murders of Nathalie's grandfather and husband, not only are these people guilty of murder, but they, or their relatives, should also be held responsible for the thefts they carried out during World War 2.'

'You're right,' agreed Perry. 'How else would they have known what was hidden? They would not be taking all this trouble and actually committing murder for the sake of recovering a few ordinary jewels. The question is, did Nathalie's grandfather realise how important that one particular object was? Surely he'd not have left it there all these years if he had.'

The conversation went on long into the night, with many different speculations and scenarios being suggested, but they concluded that there was no way anything could ever be substantiated after all this time. And neither, Ken reflected, would anyone be in a hurry to confess. As anyone involved in looting during the Second World War would now be very old, if still alive, then these people chasing Perry today must be the next generation or two, descendants of the original thieves.

As Perry returned to his vehicle, he realised that Nathalie's tent was still standing and available for him to use. He decided it would be cooler and more comfortable if he slept in it, although the overriding reason was that spending any time in what had been Nathalie's personal space comforted him. There was just the slightest trace of the *Anais Anais* perfume that she used – a light, fresh fragrance that he could sense every now and then. Before he drifted off to sleep, he prayed that she was safe now with Antony and hoped that what had become an onerous and dangerous task would soon be completed.

* * *

In the morning, Perry decided it would be safer to stay one more day, but planned to leave very early the next morning. Ken and Laurie told him they were sorry he was leaving and hoped all would go well. They themselves would be leaving in a couple of days, and Perry promised to keep in touch with the helpful couple and keep them up to date with his progress, as well as assuring them that he was safe and well.

About midday, Perry received the welcome text from Nathalie, informing him that the 'get-together' would be the next day at nine o'clock in the morning. She'd signed off as 'N'. He felt a glow of pride. What a girl! The text was bland and would mean nothing to anyone else who might read it. However, once he'd absorbed the information, he deleted the message as well as Nathalie's mobile number from his phone. He knew the number off by heart anyway. And by the time her next text arrived, it would be too late for his enemies to do anything if he was unlucky enough for his phone to fall into the wrong hands.

During the afternoon he set about dismantling Nathalie's tent, and found the job more difficult than he'd anticipated. Pitching and dismantling tents was a lot harder than it looked, yet Nathalie had made it seem so easy and had accomplished the feat all on her own. Obviously, practice makes perfect, he judged ruefully.

Once again, Laurie and Ken kindly provided an evening meal for him, and he enjoyed several hours in their company. Because he planned to leave very early in the morning, they all said their goodbyes and promised to keep in touch. He assured the friendly couple that he'd keep them informed about the success of their mission once the diamond had been returned to the museum, and felt in good spirits as he returned to his van, still sheltered in the bushes, for the night. What a relief it had been to know that Nathalie had arrived safely and was now out of danger at the house of his good friend, Antony.

EIGHT

Once she was actually driving on the main route between Tripoli and Athens, Nathalie began to relax. She had hated the idea of leaving Perry behind and possibly having to face their pursuers on his own without any help. She was now sure in her own mind that they had been responsible for both her grandfather's and her husband's deaths. She shivered as a terrible thought entered her mind and filled her body with a cold chilliness; if they'd been guilty of killing once, why would they hesitate about getting rid of Perry if and when they finally realised that he'd baulked all their plans!

Then she relaxed slightly. Perry was no fool, and would be sure to stay clear of this toxic gang – wouldn't he? That these people had already proved themselves ruthless in their quest to regain possession of this particular artefact, once again asserted itself and sent an icy splinter of fear into her mind, causing her to shiver with doubts. She could still recall the cold feeling in her heart when the tall man had stared at her just as she was leaving the campsite. She had felt his eyes boring into her skull as if he was trying to read her mind. Still trembling, she thought of how these people had robbed her of the two dearest members of her family and caused the most terrible crisis of her entire life. If she were to lose Perry as well! The whole idea was too dire to even consider. Even as she shut her mind to the distressing thought, a cold finger of fear still lingered in her heart.

She reached Corinth by mid evening, and as she pulled into a service station for fuel, she decided it would be a good idea to phone Perry's friend, Antony. After all, she thought, it would be better if he knew she was on her way to him. Better an unexpected guest than arriving in the middle of a dinner party – or some intimate situation!

Fortunately, Antony answered her call. Not knowing just how to introduce herself, she stammered, 'You don't know me, but my name is Nathalie Etienne …'

A warm, friendly male voice with only a slight accent, assured her, 'But I *do* know who you are! Perry has been in touch with me recently and told me he might need my help. Oh, yes, he told me *all* about you. But I am very intrigued. Perry said you'd fill me in with the details and how I may be able to help after your arrival. Where exactly are you now?'

Nathalie felt her face grow hot and knew her cheeks had reddened. So Perry had seen fit to tell a good friend of his all about her. Surely that meant he really cared for her. She savoured the recent memory of their bitter-sweet parting, and could still feel the heat and pressure of his lips against hers, and the exhilarating closeness of their bodies as if they had become a single entity. She'd felt the rapid beating of his heart, along with her own, as their bodies pressed together …

'I'm on the main road near Corinth,' she answered, bringing her mind rapidly back to the matter in hand. 'I'm driving a hire car and need to get rid of it.'

'Oh, I see You are on your own – without Perry?'

After Nathalie had confirmed this, he continued, 'Once on the auto-route, you will soon be in Athens. My advice to you is to park up somewhere safe and easy and hire a taxi to reach me as I'm the far side of Athens in the area of Glyfada. Just note the name of the car-park and when you get here we can ring the hire company to tell them where to pick up their hire car.'

Nathalie relaxed a little. 'Thank you for the very helpful suggestion. I hope to see you soon.'

Before she realised it, she found herself ensconced in an easy chair in Antony's smart, modern apartment. She'd parked the car, had carefully noted the name and area, flagged down a taxi, shown the helpful driver Antony's address, and *voila*, here she was, admiring the view from the apartment window and drinking a welcome, fragrant coffee. Her few bags had been transferred from the taxi into Antony's spare room. And what a room! Large, light, and airy, it had a view over all the surrounding buildings and a glimpse of sea in the distance. A sumptuous double bed faced the window, and just for a moment Nathalie imagined how it would be if Perry were there to share it with her. Then she shook herself mentally; she had an important job to do and Antony was waiting for her to tell him how he could help them both. She smiled as she imagined his expression when she finally showed him the diamond. She slipped her hand inside her shoulder-bag and was instantly reassured to feel the bulk of the pouch and its valuable contents.

'Perry told me he might need my help. What is it that he wants me to do?'

Nathalie enjoyed listening to the lilt in Antony's speech, and already felt that she trusted this short, rather tubby, dark-complexioned man with his liquid brown eyes that made her think of dark honey.

'He wants you to arrange a meeting between you and me and the top officials of the National Archaeological Museum of Athens, as soon as possible The more public the meeting, the better, because I have something of priceless importance to tell them – and until I do, my life, and Perry's, are very likely in danger!'

Antony smiled at this resolutely delivered request until Nathalie insisted she had not been exaggerating and was completely serious in her claim. 'I'm so sorry, but is it really something so drastic?'

'It is, and publicity is vital. You could say that the media will be acting as witnesses.'

'Now I'm really intrigued! Whatever has Perry been up to, for goodness sake?'

Nathalie looked uncomfortable. She had already decided after all not to tell Antony that she actually had the huge diamond in her possession, hidden safely from sight in the bottom of her shoulder-bag. The less anyone knew what she was carrying, the safer she was. 'I really would rather not say any more until a meeting is arranged, but you will have the scoop – and I can promise you that it will be a huge story. If the management are reluctant to take things seriously and won't agree to an urgent meeting, tell them it's concerning the imminent recovery of the Akbar Shah Diamond. That's all I'll say for now.'

Antony could see that Nathalie had been under extreme pressure for some days, and it would be the honourable thing to respect her wishes. 'Wow, that sounds impressive. You'll have to write down that name for me.' He handed her a notepad and pen. 'Okay, I will research the top guns of the museum and arrange a meeting – tomorrow morning if possible. But now, I think you must eat and drink a little, and then go to bed and have a good night's sleep.'

* * *

Antony was true to his word, and by the time Nathalie had presented herself for breakfast, he had already been in touch with the museum.

'I've contacted the museum top brass, including the director, as well as the whole management board, and they will all be present at a meeting at nine o'clock tomorrow morning. Is that good?'

'Well, I was hoping it could have been sometime today, but I suppose that would be expecting too much … so, well yes, that's brilliant. Thank you, Antony.' Nathalie tried to smile gratefully. She noted the questioning expression in the warm brown eyes that regarded her so closely and added, 'I must send a text to Perry to let him know when this meeting is to take place. He needs to be kept up to date.'

'Nobody seemed very keen or interested at first,' Anthony told her. 'It seemed that everyone important had other engagements lined up. It was only after I'd mentioned …' he consulted his notepad, 'the "Akbar Shah" diamond bit, that suddenly everyone was galvanised and started talking at once and the meeting agreed! The diamond's name seemed very significant to all the people concerned – in fact I would describe a definite air of excitement amongst some of the museum's experts, although I also sensed an air of scepticism from a few.'

'What about television and media coverage?' Nathalie asked anxiously.

'I'll get busy and ring some of my pals and other contacts. Don't worry, there will be enough coverage to satisfy you both!'

* * *

When at last the meeting took place, the atmosphere was quite calm, despite having previously bordered on the absolutely chaotic. Nathalie was finally seated alongside Antony and surrounded by the top officials of the National Archaeological Museum. She noted the almost hostile expressions on a few faces as the officials impatiently waited for her to speak. Wordlessly, she reached into her bag and placed the weathered pouch on the table in front of her. She was still very conscious of many sceptical pairs of eyes coldly examining her, some even sporting expressions of disapproval, as if they'd already decided that their valuable time was being wasted A few pairs of more curious eyes examined the shabby pouch lying in front of them with interest.

At last she spoke. 'What can you tell me about the Akbar Shah diamond, Messieurs?' she asked them, her eyes quickly scanning the faces surrounding her.

When some of the people present audibly sighed or tutted with impatience, she added, 'Please humour me, for I promise I'm not wasting your time.'

One of the officials, with a rather long-suffering expression on his face, finally decided to answer her question.

'It would take too long to describe the lengthy history of the diamond, Madame, but that particular artefact was, we understand, looted by someone in the German army during the Second World War, and has since disappeared completely. During the conflict, many museums, including ours, were able to move their artefacts to secret places of safety, but the Germans obviously discovered the storage area deep in the countryside of the Peloponnese where the gem was hidden. Its whereabouts today are totally unknown, and have been unknown for more than sixty years.'

'Thank you,' Nathalie replied. 'Well – unknown, until today!'

She gently tipped out the contents from the pouch – the huge diamond totally eclipsing the other gems in brilliance, its many facets reflected shafts of dazzling light as it rolled gently onto the table.

'*Voila, messieurs!* The Akbar Shah diamond, I believe.'

After she'd spoken, there was a collective gasp from her audience. Next to her, Antony uttered an incredulous exclamation and turned to stare at her with shocked eyes. Trying to ignore his reaction, Nathalie added slowly, 'I am happy to say that, after discovering this item, I have now officially returned it to the rightful owners – you – the people who represent this museum.'

As she finished speaking, there was a loud babble of voices as everyone present wanted to examine the huge diamond to check its authenticity.

Antony's cameramen were soon busy shooting pictures of the gem as well as frantically recording the whole transaction for the evening's scoop, as Nathalie had agreed. She sat back in her chair and sighed with relief. How glad she felt to be rid of the diamond, and the other gems too, that had caused her so much grief. She doubted her grandfather ever knew exactly what he'd hidden away, was certain he was unaware that he'd been in possession of a fabulous artefact that belonged in a museum to be admired by everyone, and not just another treasure to be stashed away in an avaricious, rich man's private collection But now, at last, it was back where it belonged, and she felt a sense of achievement, accompanied by a feeling of peace. Surely she had achieved what her grandfather would have wished her to do? She stretched, and let all the tension leave her body. If *only* Perry would contact her and let her know he was now safely on his way to Athens.

* * *

Later, Antony showed Nathalie a copy of the evening paper carrying the story. True to his word, she had been carefully screened from the photographs, the main picture being a close-up of the glorious jewel itself.

'As agreed by my colleagues who work for the television channel, so as to allow my paper to scoop the main story, there will only be a brief announcement of the event in tonight's news, but tell Perry that there will be full and detailed coverage on every television and radio news channel tomorrow evening.'

Nathalie glanced at Antony. 'I hope you understand why I didn't mention to you before that the diamond was actually in my bag. In truth, the possession of it has been freaking me out, and I can't begin to tell you how relieved I am to be rid of the thing.'

Antony grinned. 'It's okay. I was just a bit shocked when you produced something as fabulous as that diamond. To realise that something so famous had been right under my nose for a day or more was, to say the least, quite surprising!'

* * *

Nathalie was worried because she'd not been able to contact Perry. Although he'd responded briefly to her message the day before, there had been no further communications. She'd sent the latest text, in the agreed format, as soon as the meeting had been concluded, but there had still been no response from him. To avoid any risks, he'd already instructed her not to attempt to phone him and to wait until he called her. But there had been no message at all so far.

'I suppose it is too much to enquire how you came to know where this wonderful artefact was hidden?' Anthony enquired hopefully. 'Is there any comment you want to make? Just between the two of us, of course, about how it all happened?'

Nathalie glanced at his honest open face. Then she looked away through the large windows at the view before her, the blackness of the night decorated with strings of street lights, the glowing windows in tower-blocks, houses, and shops, and the ever-moving beams of light thrown by the still relatively heavy traffic. Looking back at Antony again, she smiled – and he was beguiled once again by her beauty, characterised by both her inner strength and her delicate, classically formed features.

She said thoughtfully, 'Let's just say that both Perry and I were doing something that my darling grandpapa would have been proud of, and something that I believe he would have wished to do himself, if he'd had the opportunity.'

After a long silence, she added, 'I'll try another text to Perry to see if he'll answer me – maybe he's driving here as we speak and it isn't safe to answer his mobile. I'll call the campsite tomorrow, anyway. If the people that helped us, Laurie and Ken, are still there, I'll also tell them to watch the evening news on the television for the full report.' Her voice contained a lilt of happiness and relief that Antony had not heard before. He smiled warmly at the courageous, beautiful woman sitting opposite him. He could easily understand how this lovely French girl had managed to melt the ice inside his good friend Perry's heart.

By late in the evening, Nathalie's insides were knotted with tension and her heart felt as heavy as a lump of ice; despite her repeated texts, there had still been no response from Perry. In desperation she had disobeyed his earlier instructions and attempted to call him, but now it seemed the number was unobtainable. She decided to confide her fears to Antony.

'Did I tell you before that a group of Germans were chasing us? They knew what we were looking for and were after the diamond for themselves. I'm terrified that these people actually caught up with Perry after I left.'

Antony's face creased with concern. 'No, you didn't tell me that.'

'Perry's mobile number seems to be unobtainable. If he got away safely, he should be *here* by now. If only I had Ken and Laurie's number,

I could call them. At least they could have told me if and when Perry left the campsite. I tried ringing the site number but there's no answer. Spiro has obviously shut the office and gone home, it's so late.' She paused and took a deep breath before adding, 'I should have told you before, but we believe the people chasing us were also responsible for murdering my grandfather – and my husband!' She was almost hysterical by the time she'd finished speaking.

Trying not to display the shock that this last statement caused him, Antony put a comforting arm around Nathalie's shoulders. 'Let's give him until the morning to arrive. If he's not here by then, well, I think we'd better get some help and try and find him. He's very resourceful, my good friend Perry, and I'm sure he'll be here soon.'

Buoyed up by Antony's reassurances, Nathalie lay in bed later and tried to imagine how wonderful it was going to be when Perry finally arrived. Then she checked herself. Was she reading too much into one passionate kiss? Did he have the same feelings for her as she had for him? *Yes, I'm sure*, she finally admitted to herself. *And I love that man with every fibre of my body! All I want is to spend the rest of my life with him, to make him as happy as I am when he's near me. I want to eradicate that sadness in his eyes caused by the loss of his boys, and fill his life with fun and laughter – and love! Lots and lots of love!*

NINE

They came for him just before dawn. One minute Perry was sleeping deeply, dreaming of Nathalie, and the next he was suddenly wide awake feeling the steely coldness of a gun muzzle against his temple, a hand clamped firmly across his mouth and powerful arms restraining him as he was pulled upwards into a sitting position. He recognised the tall man who had visited the campsite several days ago; he seemed to be in charge.

'Do as we tell you and you will come to no harm,' Perry was warned.

The man ordered him to put some clothes on, and once dressed, still at gunpoint he was forced into the driving seat of his vehicle. As he started the engine and drove along the bumpy track to the exit, the Germans crouching down out of sight, he wondered if Ken and Laurie had heard the sound of him leaving. Then his heart sank as he remembered they'd said all their goodbyes the previous night. They would naturally believe he'd made the very early start that he'd told them he intended doing, and would therefore not be at all suspicious of his rapid departure.

First he was made to drive towards the outskirts of Sparta and onto a derelict building site randomly scattered with a variety of dilapidated industrial units. Here, one of his captors jumped out and unlocked a padlock on a battered metal door through which Perry was obliged to drive his van.

The first thing his captors did was order him to hand over the information or map he'd found in his van. There were four of them – all Germans, he presumed. At this stage of the proceedings he could see no point in delaying any further, so he'd willingly searched in his shorts pocket and passed the tattered map to them without incurring any chance of receiving a thump. Only too quickly they'd identified the map as a rough drawing of the ruins of Mystras and asked him if he'd visited the old city yet and whether he had begun his search. He decided to admit that he had been to Mystras on just the one occasion, but hadn't been able to decipher the symbols on the map. He thought that they had probably believed his answer once they had spent a few minutes studying the complexities of the crudely drawn map for themselves. After that, they'd sat him on the floor, tethered his hands tightly behind his back and roped him to one of the structure's sturdy support beams.

He tried to listen to their conversation, but his knowledge of German was not good. He thought someone referred to the tall man as 'Hans', but wasn't sure. However, he picked up the word 'Mystras' a few times and it seemed to be confirming the location as they peered at the map. As it was so early, Perry wondered if they were waiting for the old city ruins to be opened to the public for the day.

After a few hours, when all Perry had been given was a bottle of water to drink, they bundled him back into his vehicle, and this time the tall man drove while another man sat in the back with him. They did not go very far. As the driver parked the vehicle towards the rear of a large area of plateau, Perry recognised the car parking area outside the old city of Mystras; so, he had been correct in his assumption. The two younger members of the team pulled up alongside in their own vehicle and jumped out. With the four men surrounding him, his hands were untied and he was pulled roughly from the vehicle. Landing awkwardly on the ground, he felt his ankle twist uncomfortably, but having at least two guns surreptitiously trained on him, he decided not to complain.

The tall man told him coldly, 'We are now entering the old city. Any trouble from you when we are buying the tickets, or at any time at all, we will kill you.'

Looking into the chill of the pale-blue eyes of his captor, Perry believed him! As the group crowded into the small entrance building along with other early tourists, and the man he had nicknamed as 'Cold Eyes' was purchasing their entry tickets, the pleasant Greek youth in the ticket kiosk spotted Perry, smiled, and commented, 'Oh, you are back again. I think you like our old city and want a second look. But your pretty lady is not with you today?'

'Er, no. Not today,' Perry was forced to respond, wishing the young man at the other side of the world.

'Cold Eyes', an even grimmer expression on his face and a sharp gleam in his glacier-like eyes as he digested this new information, hustled Perry through to the outside of the building. Once clear of the ticket office he snarled, 'A pretty lady? You were with someone else when you came here, weren't you? I knew I was right to bring you along with us and now it seems you've not been telling us the truth at all.'

Perry felt a splinter of ice pierce his heart. 'Oh, it was just a girl I met on the site,' he blustered. 'Nobody significant, but she insisted on tagging along. She's long gone now and no; she didn't know about the map.' Then it occurred to him to use this confession as an excuse. 'It's why I couldn't really concentrate on trying to find anything because the woman kept pestering me to go where she wanted to go – and she never stopped talking. I had already planned to come back on my own.'

'Cold Eyes', his face relaxing into its customary severe expression, uttered a sceptical 'Hmm', pulled Perry's mobile from his own pocket – it had been one of the first things they'd taken from him – and called up Perry's index of numbers. Perry felt a glow of relief that he'd had the foresight to remove Nathalie's details from the memory. Once the German had failed to find any entry of interest or significance, he shoved the mobile deep into his trouser pocket without any further comment. Perry thought about the meeting that would soon be taking place during the morning, and hoped that 'Cold Eyes' wouldn't trash his mobile before the all-important text from Nathalie arrived.

Once again, Perry definitely heard the older man refer to the tall man with the icy blue eyes as Hans, and Perry thought one of the two younger men addressed him as 'Vater' or something similar. Didn't that translate as 'father'? If so, were his captors a family group? If only he knew their surname. Then, if he ever managed to escape, perhaps there would be a chance that, with Ken's help, the authorities would be able to identify the group and trace these unscrupulous people. But without that vital piece of information, or any photographs, the police wouldn't stand a chance of charging them with their crimes.

As Perry and Nathalie had done a few days ago, the group stood outside the entrance building and speculated as to which footpath to follow.

'I think it's either the path to the right or straight ahead,' Perry volunteered, in a ploy to delay the proceedings. Hadn't Nathalie's text told him that the meeting would start at nine o'clock this morning? Once her next text came through, confirming a successful, well-publicised transfer of the jewel, he could stop playing for time. He needed now to be vigilant, listen carefully, and ensure that Hans decided to read the text when the mobile signalled it had arrived. At the moment his phone was likely to stay ensconced deep inside his captor's trouser pocket, so he hoped that Hans, or even he himself, would be able to hear the beep when it finally came through. Surely he could manage to stretch out the search long enough for the message to arrive?

He soon discovered, however, that he'd not allowed for the astuteness of one of the younger Germans, the studious-looking one with heavy-rimmed glasses. He'd been studying the map for some time and there was a ripple of excitement as he pointed to the first scrawled symbol of Saint George and the dragon. Perry couldn't follow the conversation, but 'Clever-clogs' was pointing to the path on the left.

'*Das ist der weg*,' he cried firmly, pushing his glasses securely back into place after they were knocked askew as the group huddled around the map. That was the only part of the animated conversation that ensued that Perry recognised, and his heart sank. He prayed that another snake would appear as it had done last time and maybe deter them from continuing. Who knows? One of them might suffer from a snake phobia. But no such luck this time. Not even the slightest wriggle to be seen between the stones or through the grass.

When the Germans reached the pretty little chapel of Saint George and realised there was nothing further to guide them— just as Nathalie and Perry had experienced a few days earlier – the group stood around Perry and demanded he tell them where to go next. Initially dismayed, *They don't believe my diversions. They suspect I got a lot further than I've led them to believe,* his survival instincts rapidly swung into action and he thought, *Perhaps I'd better play along, or they may decide to finish me off if they consider I'm no more use to them.*

'I think you probably need to continue to the next building – a small monastery called the Perebliptos, or Peribleptos – well something like that. I'd got as far as deciding that a flight of stairs had some significance. I'd already looked in that direction and drawn a blank. That's why I thought the map might be referring to a different building – somewhere else – but like I told you, I couldn't really search properly because the girl was with me.' He volunteered the information nervously, hoping to be believed.

The group moved slightly away from him and went into another huddle as they chewed over this new information. The rather studious man was pointing at the map and nodding excitedly in agreement with the suggestion. Once again, Perry thought he heard the word 'Vater' from one of the younger men and he was almost sure that he'd heard the tall man call the cleverer, bespectacled young man, 'Rolf'. Despite their need to concentrate on the poorly drawn symbols, the other older man still continued to threaten Perry with the gun in case he decided to risk an escape while they were preoccupied. Perry thought he'd heard the name 'Gustav' used by Hans when referring to the rough-looking character still threatening him with the gun.

'I must try and remember these names,' Perry thought. 'If I get out of this situation alive, I need to be able to help the authorities catch these people. Please, Nathalie, send the text! Surely the meeting must have finished by now.'

Finally, the tall man turned to Perry and said curtly, 'We will go this way and see for ourselves. My so–, colleague, is certain this is the correct route.'

Now Perry was sure; the man had come very close to identifying 'Clever-clogs' as his son. He wondered if there could be any chance of escaping when there were other people around – there were a few small groups of visitors walking about outside the little monastery. Then he rationalised that his actions could put innocent tourists in danger, so the risk ruled out that bright idea.

Inside the monastery once again, Perry's eyes once more wandered to the paintings, but this time he had no interest in studying them. He realised that unless Nathalie was with him, he'd lost any desire to admire the old building or any of its ancient colourful pictures.

'What do we look for?' growled Hans in his gutteral accent.

When Perry didn't immediately answer, 'Clever-clogs' said, 'This symbol of a lily has some significance, I think.'

'You need to look for a staircase,' volunteered Perry, trying to impress them that he was still useful and worth keeping alive.'

'And this symbol?' 'Clever-clogs' asked again.

'Maybe there will be one on a staircase?' Perry replied. 'Although I didn't find one.'

The group had already spotted the stairs near the northern entrance and moved back outside to examine the area for the lily symbol.

'What are all these numbers? Do you know what they mean?' demanded Hans.

Perry admitted, 'I wondered if they represented levels, or numbers of stones.' He decided to let them find out for themselves that one of the numbers referred to stairs, not rows of stones. At least, he'd keep that information until later, if events started becoming more serious. His heart ached as he considered the possibility that he'd never see Nathalie again. The dreadful thought that his time could be nearly over filled his being with an unbearable regret. All the time with Nathalie that had been wasted! They could at least have been together for a few sweet days if only he'd been brave enough and spoken of his feelings for her. And now it could be too late.

After a hot, dusty and unsuccessful stint of searching by counting stones and layers – just as Nathalie and Perry had done – the group finally admitted defeat. Hans' face was twisted with anger as he threatened Perry. 'You are playing us all for fools. There is nothing here. You are rapidly outliving your usefulness.'

Quickly, feeling fearful, Perry said, 'There is another staircase, I believe, accessed through the southern-facing door of the monastery. Perhaps we should look there.' He was relieved to see Hans' face clear as he considered the suggestion. However, it was obvious that he was fast running out of time, and if Nathalie's text didn't arrive soon enough it was curtains for him.

The group re-entered the monastery, walked through the building to the further exit, and then out again into the hot sunshine. 'Clever-clogs' became very excited when he viewed the steep flight of steps leading down to the flat grassy plateau below.

'*Vater, Onkel, sieh dir das mal an,*' he cried, pointing downwards. Although Perry didn't understand most of the sentence, he realised that the young man – Hans' son – had identified the steep staircase as an important area to search. Then he rewound the sentence in his mind. '*Onkel?*' Did that mean that Gustav and Hans were brothers? 'You're quite right about this staircase, my lad,' he thought sarcastically, 'but we got there first!'

Then Perry suddenly remembered his Plan B – the little pouch full of rubbishy trinkets that he'd so carefully pushed into the hiding place just after he and Nathalie had removed the original pouch. It had seemed a good idea at the time, but now … having seen the cruel expression in Hans' eyes, Perry was rapidly becoming very worried about the German's reaction once he deduced that Perry had been playing games with them all along. As the map had been in his possession earlier, they'd be bound to conclude that he had been the one who planted the baubles. This was the very last thing Perry had expected to happen, that he would actually be present at the time his little offering was uncovered.

'Please, Nathalie, send the text!' he prayed urgently. Surely the meeting must have been successfully concluded by now? The hours had been slipping past quickly and sun was now quite high in the sky. He decided to chance his arm and risk a few questions while Hans was taking a breather from stone-counting. After all, he probably had nothing to lose now.

'How did you find u– me so quickly?' Perry mentally slapped his wrist. He'd nearly given away the fact that he hadn't been on his own. It was as easy as that. 'You must have been watching the whole of Greece to spot the picture in the paper so quickly.'

Hans smirked. 'I suppose it can't hurt to tell you. It's not as if you will be going anywhere after we've found our prize. By fabricating a fake map for us to find, you unwittingly told us that you'd found the real information we had been looking for. You were a fool to think we could be tricked by your stupid fake map – we already knew from the past that what had been hidden was to be found here in this specific area. When your vehicle disappeared from sight in England it seems we guessed correctly that you'd not been able to resist interfering in something that was not your business. Therefore, we only had to watch the traffic in this particular region. However, you nearly fooled us with the registration number change and the alterations to its appearance. But, as it had been the only Safari to be seen around here, it was worth checking out.'

'Clever-clogs' suddenly called out a question to his father, who listened intently. He turned to Perry and snapped out, 'My so–, –

colleague – wants me to ask you if you think that one of the numbers refers to steps and not rows of stones?'

Perry felt a chill inside him as he pretended to consider the suggestion. 'I suppose it could do,' he said doubtfully. 'It's a possibility.' He secretly cursed the young German and his sharp brain for correctly interpreting the map so easily.

The men redoubled their efforts with enthusiasm, trying out the combinations as he and Nathalie had done. Perry closed his eyes and waited for the exclamation. When it came, it was obvious that 'Clever-clogs' had found the lily symbol. Although Perry couldn't follow the language, he got the drift of the discovery.

It seemed only seconds after that for them to finally extricate the small pouch from behind the stone. Although the others were avidly watching and waiting for the tall man to loosen the tie and tip the contents into his hand, Gustav still had the wit to keep the gun pointed at Perry. The eager expression on Hans' face sickened Perry to the core. Then suddenly he heard a signal from his mobile, although the sound was muffled by the tall man's clothing. Fortunately, Hans heard it too, quickly passed the pouch to his son and pulled the mobile from his pocket. After accessing the text message, his face darkened as he passed the phone to Perry and he demanded sharply, 'What does this message mean? Tell me!'

Perry read the words jubilantly: *'Exchange completed successfully. Watch TV and news media tonight for story. N.'* Feeling very nervous, he answered slowly and carefully, 'It signifies that a past wrong has been righted at last. Something that had been stolen years ago has been returned to the legitimate owners.'

Hans snatched the phone from Perry's hand, raised his arm and threw it hard towards a cluster of rocks. A shattering sound indicated that the mobile had been destroyed.

'You're talking in riddles!' he shouted.

Then he turned back towards Perry, whose heart had sunk at the destruction of his mobile, even though he was not in possession of it anymore. 'Now at least you'll get no more cryptic messages – or be able to call for help,' Hans snarled. 'What does it all mean? What is that message referring to? Tell me now!' His eyes narrowed to slits and his face grew black with anger, although a trace of uncertainty in his rasping voice was now clearly discernible.

'Check the contents of the pouch and see if it contains what you're actually looking for – what you expect to find,' Perry suggested bravely. Then he added more firmly, 'It's all over now. What you're looking for is back where it belongs – in Athens. That's exactly what that text meant.'

The men watched anxiously as Hans, with a face like thunder, finally tipped out the contents of the pouch into his shaking hand. Even Gustav's attention wandered from his gun as, aghast, he also viewed the cheap tacky objects that Hans was at last revealing – and at that precise moment Perry realised that this was likely to be his only chance of escape.

TEN

Almost without thinking, Perry dropped quickly over the edge of the grass plateau. After rolling uncontrollably for a distance, he then dropped about ten feet onto a narrow ledge. As he did so, he heard a shot and realised that he was now really fighting for his life. He lay still for some moments, the wind knocked out of him by the fall.

Quickly glancing round to the side of him where the sloping hillside was less steep, he could see a couple of small crumbling structures that must still be part of the ruins of Mystras. However, he rationalised that even if he hid in one of them, it would be the first place the Germans would search.

Although he realised that the ground he lay on was much steeper and more cliff-like at this point, he decided to hide in the shelter of a small crevasse and hope his pursuers would search in a different direction and be thrown off the scent. To attempt to climb down at that moment would most likely allow his enemies the chance of sighting him – and shooting. He prayed he would stay safe from view as he didn't relish the prospect of someone taking pot-shots at him while he was negotiating some tricky descent.

To his dismay, he heard sounds immediately above him and realised that the Germans were still managing to track his position. A few pebbles, dislodged by their attempts to descend too rapidly, showered down onto his head and arms. Leaving the inadequate sanctuary of his temporary shelter, he quickly dropped over the edge of the shelf and, stretching downwards, felt desperately with his feet for footholds, and cracks to grab with his hands. Moving ever faster and more recklessly in his quest to hide from his armed pursuers, he felt his left foot slipping. His grasping hands clutched wildly at the rock-face to gain some purchase, but the soft stone crumbled under his fingers, and then he was falling …

* * *

As Perry came slowly back to consciousness, he was aware of being moved. There was something really wrong with his left leg – the pain was terrible and he thought it was probably broken. Then he remembered the Germans and his rapid – too rapid – descent to escape them. The callous way he was now being pulled and shifted proved that, sadly, these were no careful paramedics in the process of rescuing him. He kept his eyes closed because he did not want whoever was carrying him to realise he was conscious, but as he listened, he could detect German being spoken, and realised that indeed, as he'd deduced, the worst had happened and his captors now had him totally within their power. He groaned, the rough handling jarring his leg with unbearable pain as they dragged him over the uneven ground. He could feel pain in his left arm too and wondered if that also was broken. Sometime later – he didn't know how much time had elapsed – he realised that the agony he'd suffered from the Germans' heedless manner of hauling him about had caused him to pass out again.

Cautiously opening his eyes a little, he could just make out that they were dragging him into one of the small stone structures he'd actually considered hiding in earlier. The daylight was still bright as he was carried into the small, tumbledown building, causing him to conclude that he'd not been unconscious for very long. When they cruelly dropped him onto the ground, he screamed with pain, and lost consciousness once more.

The next thing Perry became aware of was the tall German, Hans, leaning over him with an ugly expression on his face. He paused before asking quite mildly, 'How did you manage to transport it – the diamond – out of the area so quickly? You must have had an accomplice. The text you received today – it referred to the diamond, yes? Who sent it?

Even if Perry could have spoken, there was no way he would have volunteered any information that could implicate Nathalie.

Hans waited a moment, then, no answer being offered, sneered, 'Accomplice or not, you will suffer the same fate as the old man.' After a brief silence in which he seemed to lose all control, he shouted, 'Why did you have to be the one to purchase the Safari?' Then, almost as if he'd forgotten about Perry and was talking to himself, he said, 'After we caught the old man ...' He paused, swallowed, 'It's unbelievable! On that very night, someone actually *stole* his vehicle! He taunted us about the map and in the end he told us where he'd hidden it, before we ...'

Although he paused, he had no way of knowing the Perry realised only too well that Hans had been referring to the moment just before they'd actually killed Nathalie's grandfather. The German tried unsuccessfully to regain his composure and added wildly, his voice rasping with anger, 'We soon knew he didn't have the map on him, and then he told us where he'd hidden it ... and then ... only to find it gone!' His anger began to build again. 'Since then we've been searching and searching for it! How were we to guess the van was in Latvia, and then in England. And then to see it advertised on the Internet – and then lose our prize to *you!*'

He turned away in an effort to control his temper, and then stared coldly at Perry. 'However, we just sat in this area and waited until you arrived – and there you were. I warned you about interfering in something that didn't concern you.' His face contorted as he snarled angrily, 'Yet, despite that, you still somehow managed to evade us. You crossed us and now you will pay the price with your life. We will let the passage of time kill you now. Nobody will find you here. *Why* did you have to interfere? We *knew* the diamond was still hidden, because everyone would have heard by now if it had been recovered. That – treasure – belonged to my family and was stolen from us years ago, but for some reason the stupid person who took it had never even bothered to recover it We have spent a lot of time and trouble over the years in our efforts to regain the jewel Two people have died already because they stood in our way – and now you will be the third We even had a private buyer lined up to buy that diamond, no questions asked. You have cost us *dearly! Dearly!*'

But it wasn't yours to sell! Someone in your family stole the jewel originally, Perry thought to himself, although he felt too weak to speak aloud. *What an insanely dangerous inheritance to hand down to one's descendants. It has blighted and twisted this German family's life and turned them into cold-blooded killers, and Nathalie's grandfather has also caused his family to pay an unbearably heavy price.*

Hans' brother was busy tying Perry's feet and hands together with a strong twine. As he twisted Perry's leg to tighten the bond, the pain caused Perry to scream and yet again he blacked out into a deep faint. The next time he became conscious he was aware that it was dark and that he was alone. The killers had left him to die, as they had threatened, and gone. He shivered with pain in the sharpness of the cold night air. This was to be their revenge on him for cheating them of their prize. He tried to shift his body slightly, but the pain from his leg was excruciating. The cord around his wrists was tight and biting into his flesh. *I'm going to die,* he thought. 'I'M GOING TO DIE!' He screamed the words out as loudly as possible. But nobody came, because the old city ruins were closed for the night, and nobody ever wandered that far down the hill anyway just to look at a couple of tumbledown old houses. The only creatures that did hear the desperate cry were a few rats, mice, and night owls, momentarily disturbed by the unusual sound as they all scavenged for something tasty to eat.

* * *

Laurie and Ken were busy collecting their possessions together in preparation for their departure the next day. Although the morning sun was shining, there were some clouds making the day a bit overcast, which heralded a slightly cooler temperature.

'You know, we should really go and see the old city of Mystras before we go,' Laurie said slowly. 'I'd like to see the place, especially after Nathalie and Perry enjoyed it so much. They said the old buildings were really beautiful.'

'Well, if you'd really want to go, I suppose we could do it now,' grumbled Ken. 'But you know I'm not really into climbing around old ruined buildings!'

'I promise we'll not stay too long,' said Laurie, smiling with pleasure.

Later, after turning into the access road, they pulled onto the area set aside for parking. Although only mid-morning, there were already plenty of parked cars as well as coaches and a small minibus. To the rear of the parking area, standing higher than the cars around it, they could see the top of a white van. Ken glanced casually at the vehicle as he absorbed the general view, and then his head shot round again as he re-focused on the van once more with its distinctive rear roof rack.

'Oh, dear God, I think that could be Perry's van over there!'

Laurie's eyes followed her husband's pointing finger. 'You mean the tall vehicle right at the back? How can you tell?'

'The roof rack is quite distinctive. I'm not sure, of course, but we've got to go over there and check it out. If it proves to be Perry's van, it means he never left this area. At least, not under his own steam. This could mean that he was caught as soon as he left the campsite by the men who were chasing him earlier. If so, he must be in great danger if he never managed to escape from this area at all.'

'You don't think he's dead?' Laurie whispered, her face white with shock.

'Let's check the van first before we jump to any conclusions,' Ken said firmly.

Once they reached the van, it was plainly obvious that it was indeed Perry's pride and joy. Apart from a big dent on the driver's side, where it appeared that someone had either walloped the panel with a weapon or given the side a mighty kicking, the rest of the vehicle seemed to be undamaged. When Ken tried the back-door handle, the door opened, but a quick look round revealed there was nobody inside.

Ken stroked his chin, deep in thought. 'There's no way that Perry would have left his Safari unlocked. Whatever those men have done to him already, they surely wouldn't bother to take him with them. No, he must still be here – at Mystras. I bet they've hidden him, or his body, if it's come to that, among the ruins somewhere in this old city. We've got to find him – activate a search immediately in case he's still alive somewhere, but trapped ...'

Laurie's face had turned even paler. 'I should have said something to you yesterday, but I thought it had been my imagination.'

'Tell me now,' Ken urged.

'Well, you know I need to get up early to use the toilet. Yesterday morning I heard Perry leaving the site. I unzipped the tent just enough to peep through and saw the Safari driving by and I thought ...' she paused miserably.

'Tell me!' Ken urged again, impatiently.

'I thought there might have been ... just for a moment, I thought I saw someone sitting in the back seat.' Laurie tailed off unhappily. Then she added, 'But it was still quite dark, and you know how bad my eyes are – I thought it had been a trick of the light shining on the window.'

The anxious couple hurried to the ticket office and waited until the young Greek behind the counter had dealt with a group of tourists.

Ken approached the man. 'Do you recall an Englishman, short, toffee-coloured hair, in his thirties, who visited you yesterday? He could have been with a group of people.'

'The man who came with his beautiful girlfriend just a couple of days before?' When Ken nodded, he continued, 'Yes, I remember him, because I asked him where she was. Such a lovely girl. Yesterday, he was with some men – I think Germans or Austrians maybe.'

'Do you remember him leaving Mystras?' Ken enquired anxiously.

'No, I was watching for him. But I did notice the four men leave.

I thought at the time that they were behaving rather strangely.'

'How so?' enquired Ken, carefully noting the fact that there were at least four members in the gang.

The young man scratched his head as he tried to recollect why he had originally formed that impression. 'In the first place, your friend was not with them, which I thought was odd. Then they seemed to be trying to avoid being noticed by mixing in with a coach-load of tourists who were leaving at the same time. They just seemed to be behaving rather – what you would say – furtively.'

The Greek looked uncomfortable as he added, 'Those people he was with – they were not like tourists, not so nice, and your friend looked – unhappy – to be with them. That is why I looked for him later and am certain he didn't leave with them. However, I decided that I *must* have missed his departure somehow, if he had left separately.'

Ken's face was grim. 'His vehicle is still parked outside. Those four men are dangerous. I think he's been hurt – or worse. He could have been hidden in one of the old buildings since then, trapped and unable to escape.'

Almost before he'd finished speaking, the young Greek had picked up his phone and was making some very urgent calls.

* * *

The rest of day passed in a welter of confusion. All the buildings in the ancient city were being searched, not only by police; many tourists already present on the site joined in the hunt. Ken telephoned Spiros, the campsite owner, who then conscripted a number of people from the campsite, and soon, as well as the larger buildings being carefully searched, a line of people set about scouring the hill and rocks below the city.

After several hours, one of the tourist searchers shouted, 'Down here, below the rocks! There is a shoe here! I don't think it's been here long.' He reached down and held up a well-worn black trainer.

A dozen or more people climbed carefully down the easier slopes of the hillside and began to comb the area more diligently. Someone pointed to a couple of small ruins, and a group of people hurried over towards them.

'He's here! He's here!' shouted one of the tourists excitedly. 'I think he's still alive!'

* * *

Falling into ever longer periods of unconsciousness, and completely losing all sense of time, Perry eventually became aware of voices all around him. First he was deliriously fantasising that he was listening to a choir of angels, then as he became more fully aware, he realised that they were real voices and calling his name. Opening his eyes, he could see that once again there was daylight, signifying that the endless night had at last passed. And now there were people out there searching for him and this could be his only chance of attracting their attention. Gathering all his strength, he shouted, 'I'm here!' but in reality all he could manage was a faint whisper. *They'll never find me*, he thought tearfully as once again he drifted into oblivion.

By the time the group of excited searchers eventually discovered him just a few moments later, he was once again deeply unconscious.

* * *

After that, everything speeded up as first of all a doctor examined the unconscious man, then ambulance-men carefully placed his injured body onto a stretcher. Many hands assisted in transferring the stretcher smoothly to the path above. With Ken and Laurie beside him in the ambulance, Perry was efficiently whisked off to the nearest fully equipped hospital in Kalamata.

After some hours of waiting anxiously outside the ward, a doctor made his way over to the tired, worried couple.

'You are friends of the patient, Peregrine Smithieson?'

Ken answered, 'Well, yes, we are. But we only know him as Perry, we didn't know his surname. Smithieson, eh?'

The doctor smiled wearily. In his strongly accented English he told them, 'The police found his passport inside the American vehicle. That's how we know his name. However, I can tell you that although Mister Smithieson was seriously dehydrated after being tethered and abandoned for at least a day without food or water, and in addition had also suffered a broken tibia – leg – and a dislocated shoulder from some sort of fall, he is now responding well to treatment. He is in good shape overall and – well – we are certain he will soon be on the mend.'

Ken smiled broadly. 'That is really good news.'

The doctor added, 'Your friend also suffered a multitude of minor cuts and bruises, but he is young enough to make a good recovery very soon.'

Laurie asked tentatively, 'Can we see him?'

The doctor shook his head. 'He's under sedation and will shortly be going to theatre for an operation on his leg. It will be better if you rest, and come back tomorrow morning.'

* * *

It was already dark by the time the exhausted couple arrived back at the campsite. As they reached the entrance, Spiros rushed from his home and indicated that he wanted to talk to them both. Ken parked beside the house and laboriously extricated himself from the driving seat. The excited campsite owner cried, 'The young lady, Nathalie! She called me. She says we all need to watch the evening news on television. Come in! Come in! The news will start very soon. I have been watching for you for many hours, and you are just in time.'

'We've been at the hospital,' Ken explained. 'Perry is responding well to treatment, and his leg will be operated on this evening.'

'I told the young lady about Perry, and she is on her way back here,' Spiros informed them. 'She is very worried about her man.'

'Oh, I don't think Perry is her man exactly,' Laurie explained.

'They're just very good friends.'

'Oh yes he is!' Ken interrupted, contradicting her firmly. 'He's very *definitely* her man all right!'

Laurie gave her husband a strange look and wondered how he'd come to such a positive conclusion.

The item they were waiting for was prime news that night. Ken's eyes sharpened as the subject was introduced. 'This is undoubtedly what she wants us to listen to,' he confirmed.

With Spiros rapidly interpreting as the report progressed, they heard the first, full, detailed television interview with the director of the National Archaeological Museum of Athens as he announced that they had, as already reported in the press, and more briefly on television the previous day, recovered an important and priceless artefact that was believed stolen during the Second World War and had been missing ever since. Now, a day later, the artefact's identity was officially confirmed as the huge, pear-shaped, colourless diamond, seventy-one carats in weight, called the Akbar Shah diamond. Its origins were in the Mughal Dynasty, Persia, and it is believed to be part of the original Peacock Throne. The director went on to say that the diamond had been returned to the museum by a young couple, who wished to remain anonymous, who had discovered its whereabouts in the ancient, ruined city of Mystras on the Peloponnese.

A picture of the hugely impressive diamond was shown on the screen as the director was still talking. Then an expert on diamonds went on to explain how it had disappeared more than sixty years ago and all hope of ever finding it had faded. After that the talk became technical as the expert expounded on the beauties and virtues of this particular specimen.

Spiros scratched his head in puzzlement. 'All very interesting, but what has this to do with us? Why would Nathalie wish us to see this?'

Ken cleared his throat before answering. 'Because she and Perry were the couple who actually located the diamond in the ruins of

Mystras, and because Nathalie is the young lady referred to in the reports, who returned the diamond to the Museum. Unfortunately, Perry has been the victim of the group of unscrupulous Germans who wished to keep the diamond for themselves.'

A bewildered and shocked Spiros uttered a loud expletive in his native language, the rudeness of which his two listeners could only assume!

'This diamond was hidden in Old Mystras for all these years?' he finally queried, shaking his head in disbelief.

'Apparently so,' Ken replied, 'but that's all I know. We must wait for Nathalie's return to find out more details.'

ELEVEN

Now in the busier part of the season, the campsite just outside the town of Sparta was buzzing with people camping in every type of accommodation that could be imagined, from the most luxurious motor caravans to the tiniest of tents. The pool resounded with shrieks of excitement from children on their summer holidays; laughter, the buzz of conversation, and the splashing sounds of much water being strenuously displaced.

Perry lay on a sun lounger in the shade of a pine tree, inhaling the fragrance exuding from the branches above him. He watched the sun attempting to stab a multitude of shifting shards of diffused light through the dense pine needles, the branches wafting a gentle heat in the mid-afternoon breeze. He felt the warmth kissing his limbs when the rays from time to time touched his skin. It was pleasant to be able to simply rest and think about all the recent events without worrying about violent thugs, diamond artefacts, or, indeed anything else. The pulsating chirping of cicadas created an almost hypnotic sensation which caused him to feel sleepy and relaxed.

Spiros, ever helpful and supportive, had arranged for the Safari to be collected by his brother, who owned a garage in Sparta. The dent in the side of the vehicle had been repaired and the Safari looked as good as new again. Perry had no doubt how the damage had been done. He could just imagine one of the murderous, frustrated gang of killers spitefully delivering a hefty kick to his beloved vehicle. He knew only too well just how frustrated and furious they had been when they realised all chance of ever regaining possession of the huge diamond had been completely lost. After all, they'd vengefully left him, injured and helpless, to die a miserable death on his own. He idly wondered if they knew by now that their plan had failed and that he'd not died, as intended, but been discovered and rescued before it was too late.

He glanced to his right and could see Laurie and Ken Wilding sitting to the side of their outfit. They were in serious conversation with Nathalie and Antony, and Perry knew what was still worrying them; the German gang's presence was still unaccounted for. Although they'd purposely left him on his own to rest, he was finding it very difficult to relax sufficiently to find sleep. *Anyway,* he told himself, *I am resting my leg and shoulder even if sleep is eluding me.* His eyes were drawn to Nathalie as she sat talking to the others. He could only see the profile of her lovely face as she turned towards Antony and regretted how serious she appeared. Well, it would be his aim, for the future, to ensure that she would be so happy that her lovely mouth would forever curve into her gorgeous smile and the light would always shine from her expressive eyes – as he had been lucky enough to witness before the dreadful episode.

He smiled to himself as he thought about what had been happening since he left the hospital. Laurie and Ken had insisted on staying in Sparta and helping Nathalie look after him until he was fully recovered. After all the traumatic events they had shared, both Nathalie and he now felt a strong bond with the older couple. They were like the parents that neither Nathalie nor he had anymore. Technically, they each still had a parent living, but by coincidence each had chosen to settle the other side of the world and were no longer an important part in either of their offspring's lives. Not only that, but Perry felt an immense debt of gratitude to Ken as, if he hadn't been so watchful, he, Perry, would certainly have died. Nobody ever ventured into that area of the ruins and people would not have been close enough to hear his ever-weakening voice calling for help. The police had admitted it was doubtful he would ever have been discovered in time but for Laurie's and Ken's insistence that he'd never left – never been *allowed* to leave – the ancient old city.

Perry recalled the first time Nathalie had visited him in the hospital. She had rushed in, Antony trailing behind her, and kissed and hugged him as much as was possible, her eyes filled with tears and a big smile lighting her lovely face.

'Oh, Perry, are you all right? I 'ave been so worried!' In her fear and distress, her accent as ever was much more clearly in evidence.

In truth he was feeling much better. His shoulder *had* been dislocated by his fall but that had soon been put right and now it was as good as new, or almost. However, having a leg in a plaster cast was a more difficult problem to deal with.

'Oh, I'm good, especially now you're back safe and sound!'

Nathalie had half turned away to hide the tears running down her face. '*Mon Dieu*, Perry, I thought I 'ad lost you! Sometimes it seems as if everyone I love is taken away from me and I thought it 'ad happened all over again!'

'Everyone you *love*?' he'd teased her, his heart suddenly beating much faster.

Her face had reddened as she realised how much of her true feelings she had revealed to him. And then she had stood straight and declared bravely, 'Yes. *Everyone* I love!'

With his undamaged arm, Perry had pulled her towards him, and as she sat down on his bed, he drew her face towards his own. 'That's just as well,' he'd whispered in her ear, 'because I love you too! I won't ever let you slip away from me now. We've got a lot of unfinished "business" to discuss. Just you wait until I'm out of this plaster!'

'Oh, Perry,' Nathalie had sobbed. 'I thought I'd left it too late to tell you just how much I care for you. I was so *convinced* it was all *much* too late.'

'Well, don't cry, my love. Be happy now. We've got a future to plan because I don't intend for us to part ever again.' Then he'd added, with a twinkle in his eyes, 'Besides your tears are making me so wet, I might drown.'

His mild attempt at humour had the desired effect because Nathalie sat up and looked deep into his eyes, her brilliantly flame-coloured hair framing her delicate features. 'I'm crying because I'm so 'appy – not sad. I am so 'appy you are alive and will soon be well again.'

Antony, who had been standing tactfully by the door, now moved towards his bed. 'You really got yourself into a situation this time, my old friend. Why dabble with trivia when you could really do something important,' he'd joked weakly.

Perry had smiled gratefully back.

'You could say that a certain American vehicle was the one to blame for all this activity. Mind you, the Safari did enable me to find Nathalie, and I'm very grateful for that. Without my Internet purchase, I'd never have met her. What an awful thought!'

Antony had looked puzzled by this statement.

'Nathalie only told me of your incredible find at Mystras. I thought it had been a chance find – a lucky fluke. Is there more to the story?'

'Both Ken and Laurie already know about it all, but if Nathalie agrees, perhaps we should tell *you* the whole story at last. It is her right to make that decision, because most of it concerned her in the first place.'

Nathalie had smiled tremulously and nodded her assent. And so it was agreed that after Perry returned to Spiros's campsite to recuperate, they would tell the whole story to the trusty Greek journalist who had been unexpectedly caught up in the drama. And as Perry picked up his crutches with the intention of joining the group, he decided that now was exactly the right time to tell Antony at last …

* * *

More than an hour later, the sorry tale had been told. Antony was stunned by all the details, and Laurie, with tears in her eyes, wrapped her arms around Nathalie. 'Oh, you poor darling!' she exclaimed. 'Although Perry has already told us the story of what went on before his kidnapping, I can feel your pain once again. To lose both your grandfather and husband in such awful circumstances, it breaks my heart to think of it. What cruel, ruthless people those men were.'

Hearing Perry tell the story again also brought back to Nathalie memories of the whole disastrous episode, and the pain she'd suffered at the time. With emotion she said, 'If only the police had been able to catch the murderers, it would have 'elped me to gain some closure. I don't think the police 'ave any idea who to search for, their names or even what they looked like. We saw the man who called at the campsite, and Perry was at close quarters with all of them for hours, but could any of us even begin to describe or sketch their faces?' She looked down at the ground in distress, and then added, 'We don't even know if any of the names we heard are their true names. Spiros says the tall man called himself "Hans Hausmann" when he visited the site, but how do we know it's his real name?'

At this Laurie suddenly gasped and they all turned towards her.

'Wait!' she called as she rushed into the tent behind them. After a moment, she came out carrying her camera. 'I'd almost forgotten about it until this moment,' she exclaimed, smiling nervously. 'It's a habit of mine when I'm on holiday – I am always darting around taking pictures of all and sundry. I was doing just that on the day the tall man with the cruel eyes called at the campsite and Ken wanted me to delay him from searching the site.' With a wicked smile, she said, 'Well, I did delay him a bit, but I also managed to take a couple of pictures of him!'

As the others exclaimed with excitement, she added, 'I don't think he ever suspected that I was keeping a record of his appearance – just in case. Having been married to a detective for many years does rub off, you know. I've learnt a few lessons from you, Ken!' She smiled sweetly at her astounded husband as she accessed the photos and showed them to the group.

After studying the images of the tall German with the cruel eyes for some moments, taken as he'd been talking to Spiros, Antony took charge. 'As soon as I return to Athens tomorrow, I'll take your camera and pass on these pictures to my detective inspector friend in the police force, if you agree.' He turned to Nathalie. 'With your permission, my dear, I'll tell the police the whole story – right back to what happened during the war. In due course, I expect they will need to speak to you both.'

Nathalie nodded, and Antony enquired, 'Am I right in assuming you haven't already told them about Nathalie's grandfather, Perry?'

'Yes, that's right. I wanted to ask Nathalie's permission first before telling them all that part of the tale,' Perry confirmed. 'But we'd be grateful if you'd do the honours for us now.'

Antony continued, 'Perry has already supplied information about their names to the police, and it appears that they are from one family only.'

Perry interrupted eagerly, 'I'm quite sure that the tall man's first name is Hans, and that the two younger men were his sons. I heard them call each other Rolf and Fritz – no, that's not right – Franz. I'm also sure that the other older man was Hans' brother and he was called Gustav. Anyway, yes, I did pass all this on to the police while I was still in hospital. However, it's their surname that is really the key question.'

Antony nodded. 'They should be able to check the names with the records of German soldiers stationed in Greece at that time. And with a good facial image, it should be quite easy to identify the "Hans Hausmann" individual, plus the names of his family members. You really think your grandfather took the diamond from one of his superior officers, Nathalie?'

'Well, no, I'm not really sure, but it's a possibility. He would have been very young then, still a teenager. It's an explanation and a reason why that family had been searching for my grandfather and anything connected to him – in this case, the GMC vehicle. I don't know why the people concerned took so many years to find him, or how they finally discovered his whereabouts, but they knew what he'd done, and killed him because of it. What they never found was his map.'

'From what they said to me,' said Perry, 'during the time they held me a prisoner, it does seem likely that the father – or another close relative – of Hans had committed the original theft at some point when he was your grandfather's superior officer and that Nathalie's grandfather had seized an opportunity to swipe the diamond and other jewels from him. As far as they were concerned the diamond was theirs, or their family's, and they were determined to have it. Hans as good as admitted to me that they'd been responsible for killing two people already. And that I was to be the third!'

Turning to the others he went on, 'Thank goodness they didn't connect Nathalie to their previous two victims. In fact, they seemed totally unaware of her existence. Neither were they aware that I knew or suspected what crimes they'd already committed.' Glancing at Nathalie, he then added gently, 'I don't think for a moment that your grandfather realised the significance of one of the items he'd taken. He probably thought that his seniors wouldn't even notice the absence of a few baubles. It seems there were other artefacts they were also probably responsible for stealing at the same time – perhaps we'll never know how many.' As Nathalie confirmed his thoughts by nodding, he continued, 'Goodness knows how the original thieves identified your grandfather as the culprit who'd helped himself to their haul, but over all these years they *did* know exactly *who* they were looking for. It was his bad luck that they finally caught up with him …'

* * *

Lying close together on the rather uncomfortable bed in the small chalet that Spiros had kindly made available for him, Perry shifted himself so that he could reposition his good arm around Nathalie. He'd never realised just how wonderful and satisfying it could be lying so close to his love, to be able to touch and caress and love her, even if technically she was not yet his lover. For the time being, Nathalie was still sleeping in her trusty old tent. With Perry's leg still in plaster, it was difficult enough for him to get a decent night's sleep, but he was already counting the days until its removal.

However, lying together for a few hours each day was wonderful enough. Kissing and embracing each other, they spent happy hours whispering their plans for the future while their hearts beat fast with the knowledge and anticipation of the time when their bodies would at last be able to lovingly cleave together without any barriers – when they could at last become as gloriously close as two mortals could ever be. Although they were both impatiently counting the days when they could finally give themselves purely and naturally to each other, they both felt a peacefulness and a sense of inevitability about their future union, which helped to counter their natural sexual cravings.

Now, as Perry lost himself in the fathomless depths of Nathalie's eyes, he gloried in the knowledge that his emotions were so wonderfully reciprocated. He heard Nathalie sigh with pleasure, and as he felt her lips touching his cheek and the warmth of her breath on his skin, he felt humbled by the fate that had somehow brought them together. And once again he marvelled at the diversity of events that had brought him this beautiful woman, who would henceforth always be part of his life.

TWELVE

Although it was still early when Perry awoke, he could already see bright stripes of sunlight painted on the bedroom wall opposite, and hear the twittering and piping calls of house martins as they roosted in the shady eaves of Nathalie's little house.

Turning over to his left, he could see she was still out for the count. She was breathing quietly, little puffs of air warm against his skin as he leaned over to kiss her soft cheek. The half-moons of her dark lashes trembled as she shifted her position slightly, and he admired the wonderful curve of her generously shaped lips, and longed to kiss them passionately – but it would be mean to wake her up just yet!

They had been very busy for the last week or so, hunting for a new home. It had involved a lot of walking – down secret tracks and along quiet lanes, as well as tramping around the extensive grounds that some of the properties boasted. This trip had been to the region of south Dordogne and they were hopeful that this might be the right area at last, although the property of their dreams had not yet turned up. They had already viewed some lovely houses, but some were just too big, or too small, others had too many hectares of land, or not quite enough. Or perhaps it was purely that they'd not yet managed to find the house with the special, indefinable quality they were hoping for.

Although used to plenty of exercise, Perry could still feel a slight tension in his calves, especially in his previously broken leg – but what an enjoyable trip it had been, though they'd arrived home very late last night, early in the morning in fact, quite exhausted.

It was now almost a year since they had ventured into Greece, located the famous diamond and returned it to The National Archaeological Museum in Athens. After some serious discussion,

Perry had happily agreed to sell his home in England and move into Nathalie's sweet little village house in France. He was now remembering the first time they made love. Although they'd waited until all his injuries were healed, it had been as wonderful and fulfilling as he'd ever imagined it could be. Loving Nathalie seemed to have an inevitable rightness about it, as if they'd always been meant to be together. The depth of his feeling for her was immeasurable, and anyone only needed the briefest look at Nathalie these days to see how deliriously happy *she* was!

Since Perry had moved in, Nathalie had even returned to some part-time teaching, acting as a supply teacher to be called upon when necessary, but Perry knew that she was really counting the days and dreaming of the time when she would become pregnant. So far they had been unsuccessful, but Perry constantly reassured her that it was still early days.

Even so, they gloried in their attempts to be successful. Just the very thought of the wonderful, miraculous possibility of a baby being created at the moment when their bodies were bonded so tightly together added an indescribable piquancy to their lovemaking. This excitement was a shared emotion, because although Perry had experienced the wonder of becoming a father already, he'd never before felt this almost primitive hunger to create a baby with his beloved Nathalie. Of course, Nathalie had been pregnant when she was married to Bernard, but she'd lost the baby while still in the early stages, and now he knew how much her body craved to absorb *his* seed that would flower from the combined essence of them both. Then they would share with each other their very own personal miracle when their baby finally arrived.

He remembered how, during their time in Greece, she had grown angry at the cruel way his ex-wife had been able to deprive him of his two boys. Unless there was day-to-day contact with children, it was always inevitable that they would gradually grow apart. His only hope was that his boys would choose to seek him out more often once they became adults. So far they had been inveigled to come over for a visit during the late summer, and not only did they seem to enjoy themselves immensely, but they also got on really well with Nathalie. Because of this feeling of separation from his sons, he realised just how important it now was to Nathalie to successfully fill the awful void in his life with their own child. However, he didn't view it quite like that – a child or children with Nathalie would be wonderful and precious to him not to fill a vacuum in his life but simply because – well – *Nathalie* would be their mother. He'd tried to convince Nathalie of this fact, but knew that she still felt his pain when the time came to return his boys to Pamela.

Selling his house in England had been easy enough because he'd instructed the estate agents to drop the selling price if they considered the viewers to be serious buyers who could proceed quickly with the purchase. Learning to speak French was a much harder task, but Nathalie was always there to correct him when he made mistakes. Smiling to himself, he decided that perhaps in ten years' time he would be considered fairly fluent in the language!

The idea of moving to a different property, chosen by them both, was not only to provide a comfortable home large enough for a family if – no, when – they were blessed with children, but to provide Perry with the opportunity to farm enough animals and crops to render them virtually self-sufficient. If there was the ability to also provide a *gite* as a separate business venture, all well and good.

As he lay contentedly in bed, while the early morning sun rapidly warmed the room, he turned his mind back to the episode in Greece once again. True to his word, Antony had speedily turned over Laurie's pictures to the police. Once in possession of the gang leader's image, it had been relatively easy for Interpol to track his family via the German army's archives. Apparently 'Hans' *was* Perry's captor's true name, but his surname was really Stiebling and he'd proved to be the son of Anton Stiebling, who had served as an officer in the German army and been stationed in Greece towards the end of the war and who had died just a year ago.

When the police finally arrested the four men at their homes in Germany, they'd been totally surprised and unaware that they'd actually been identified – or that anyone had had the means to be *able* to. Perry wondered if the police had ever shown Hans the picture Laurie had successfully taken of him while she'd been darting around the campsite snapping different views. The French police had charged three of the men with the murders of Nathalie's grandfather and her husband, and the fourth, the youngest man, was charged as an accessory to both the crimes. It meant that they were all now in prison and would be there for many years to come. Apparently, Hans Stiebling had been considerably upset to realise that Perry had been rescued and had actually *survived* his ordeal, and therefore been able to aid the police in arresting him.

The authorities had told Nathalie that, although there was no actual proof, it was believed that Anton Stiebling, while an army officer stationed in Greece, had taken the opportunity to stash away a small hoard of museum artefacts taken from a collection which was destined to be sent back to the so-called Fatherland. By sheer chance, Nathalie's grandfather had discovered the senior officer's hoard and hadn't been able to resist taking a few items for himself in the last days before the whole German unit had disbanded in panic, knowing the war had been lost. It had become obvious that the Stiebling family knew exactly who had taken the artefact and all of them had been searching for their quarry ever since the war had ended.

Some other good news was that they'd received a cheque for a considerable amount of money, a thank-you gift from the authorities of the grateful Museum.

All in all, the situation had been very satisfactorily resolved, Perry thought. Then an idea popped into his mind. Surely this would be a wonderful time to revisit Greece – especially Sparta and Mystras once more. It would be easier to plan a visit before they became embroiled with all the tasks involved in moving house once they found their dream home. They could use their car and sleep in Nathalie's tent, which was more than adequate for two people As soon as Nathalie woke up, he'd see if she liked the idea.

He sighed as he recalled his beloved Safari. Once he had settled in with Nathalie in France, it had been inevitable that the vehicle would have to be sold. There were just too many bad memories and associations with an unhappy past to enjoy owning it any longer. Not that Nathalie had ever complained, but the vehicle must have stood as a constant reminder of her poor grandfather and the way he was so brutally killed. However, they now had a spacious, ruggedly capable, four-wheel drive vehicle that would serve them well on such a trip.

He turned towards Nathalie and snuggled against her, drinking in the sensation of her hair against his face and the fresh apple smell of her shampoo. She engendered feelings in him he had never experienced before – lust, passion, excitement, mixed with an overwhelming love and tenderness. Maybe more importantly, she had become his best friend, his companion, his soul-mate. He savoured the warmth of her body, lying so closely against him. Then she turned and sleepily kissed him on his lips.

'Oh, so you're awake at last, sleepyhead,' he murmured. Her answer was to pull him so tight against him that he felt the heat of her breasts against his body. Despite their late night and lack of sleep, he felt himself readily hardening in response.

'I've been awake for a few minutes, watching you and wondering what you were thinking about,' said Nathalie softly.

Surprised not to have noticed that she'd been awake and observing him, Perry said, 'Apart from admiring you and wanting desperately to kiss your luscious sleepy lips, I've had an idea and want to see what you think …'

'Not just now – carry out your first suggestion and tell me later, my love,' Nathalie whispered seductively as she wrapped her arms around him and pulled him into her, soft inviting body. Then he forgot all about Greece and trips abroad, as he lost himself once again in the magic spell and enchantment woven by the woman he loved so deeply and passionately. Just before his mind totally blew apart, as he willingly surrendered to the wonderland of sensations, his last coherent thought was, 'Perhaps this time we'll be blessed ...'

* * *

As Perry parked the car again on the familiar, rough, dusty ground of the Mystras car park, he tried to estimate the position that the GMC vehicle had been parked when he'd left it less than a year ago. Further to the rear, nearer the perimeter, he decided. He thought back to their arrival at the campsite a few days' ago. Spiros had been very happy to see them both again and it took a lot of effort to dissuade him from settling them into his own house as guests! However, they'd managed to convince him that they really *enjoyed* camping and had pitched the tent in a very pretty, shady position under a few trees. Perry's lips twitched into a secret smile as he wondered just how much kudos Spiros was gathering from the locals at having a near-celebrity, who'd nearly died in Mystras a year ago, back once more on his campsite.

He watched as Nathalie gathered her bag, sunglasses, and hat and elegantly climbed out of their vehicle. They began the walk across to the ticket office and entry gate into the old ruined city. When they arrived and joined the short queue, Perry was sorry to see that a different young man was now working behind the desk. Time moves on, he thought, and they were probably all students filling in gap years from various universities.

He glanced at Nathalie and thought once again how beautiful she was, wearing a bright patterned orange skirt topped by a skimpy black vest, and sandals, her vibrantly coloured hair topped with a smart, black, floppy sunhat. He thought she'd never looked lovelier. Her face was speckled with spots of diffused light where the sun's rays were able to penetrate through the weave of the hat's brim, and she had an almost indefinable glow of serenity and happiness radiating from her person. Perry wondered if other people sensed this quality when they saw her, and then tried to speculate as to whether he also radiated any of his joy and happiness so conspicuously, because he certainly felt he was the luckiest man alive these days.

Once inside the perimeter of the old city, Perry glanced around and felt an unexpected cold chill of fear fill his heart. Awful things had happened to him here, and as he suddenly found himself nervously examining the other sightseers and tourists, he wondered for the first time whether after all it had really been such a good idea to revisit the old city. Then he felt a warm hand slip into his own as Nathalie moved close to him.

'If this is too difficult for you, we don't have to stay,' she said quietly, squeezing his hand gently in sympathy.

Perry realised just how perceptive Nathalie was in sensing his emotions, and how much he was allowing himself to indulge in fanciful feelings.

He smiled at her, noting her concerned expression. 'I'm fine' he said firmly. 'Just a touch of the heeby-jeebies, but now I'm good.'

'What are the 'eeby-jeebies?' enquired Nathalie, and Perry laughed.

'I shouldn't expect a pretty French girl to know a word like that! It's an expression, and means a touch of the jitters.' Glancing at Nathalie's still-puzzled expression, he added, 'A few – shaky – moments.'

'Well, I expected that!' exclaimed Nathalie. 'It would be unusual if you didn't feel apprehensive. After all, you nearly died in this place. You are *sure* you want to carry on?'

'Oh yes, there're some paintings I want to spend some time looking at. I didn't get a chance last year, did I! We'll start off by turning left again and revisiting the Peri …'

Nathalie smiled and consulted the guide sheet. 'The Peribleptos,' she supplied.

'*That* building first anyway,' Perry said as they walked along the narrow, well-trodden path towards the little chapel of Saint George once again.

Nathalie shivered. 'I hope we won't surprise any snakes this time.'

Although they kept a careful lookout, they didn't disturb any wildlife on their repeat journey along the path leading to the sweet little chapel of Saint George and then onwards towards the Peribleptos monastery. They both finally stood before the ancient building and admired the view once more, taking in the sturdiness of the structure buttressed firmly against the rock face, the hill rising steeply behind to provide protection and shelter from any enemy attacks.

'Let's get inside and look at all those wonderful paintings,' Perry insisted enthusiastically, as they climbed the steps to the main entrance.

Nathalie smiled indulgently and they both hurried towards the wonderfully colourful frescoes, depicting events, or believed events, of a long-distant past.

* * *

For four busy hours they exhausted themselves climbing along steep access paths, exploring the wonderful mediaeval ruins. They were all breathtakingly beautiful and quite different in appearance. The church of the Hodegetria, and Saints Theodores, had been sympathetically restored in some parts to their original condition, and then there was the cathedral of the Metropolis, one of the most important religious monuments of Mystras, decorated with colourful frescos of religious events, and which also contained the site's museum.

They had reached the church of Evangelistria, a lovely ruin with simple plaster and ceramic decoration, when they both finally admitted defeat. Collapsing onto a tempting area of grass in a sheltered area beside one of the church's stone walls, Perry cried, 'Enough! I give in. No more for today, please!'

Nathalie gratefully sat beside him and stretched her aching legs before her. 'There's a lot we haven't seen yet,' she remarked.

'It'll have to wait for another day – or year,' Perry replied. 'My mind is crammed with visions of pictures, historical facts, and fascinating ruins. There's no room for any more details!'

Rummaging around in his small knapsack, he located a bottle of water and handed it to Nathalie. She gratefully swigged some of its contents and handed the bottle back to Perry. 'Phew, I needed that It's getting really hot now. We need to move into the shade or we'll be shrivelled up.'

They found a shady corner by the wall and sat with their backs against the warm stones. For a while they rested in companionable, drowsy silence, easing their aching muscles into comfortable positions.

After a peaceful eternity, Perry felt Nathalie's hand touch his. 'Hold me,' she whispered 'Put your arm round me just for a moment, because there's something special I want to tell you.'

Surprised by her sudden request, but only too pleased to comply, he wrapped his nearest arm around her waist as she shifted closer and turned to face him. Meeting his surprised gaze, she smiled, the mysterious, secretive, age-old smile of a woman truly fulfilled.

'Don't look so worried, my love.' She looked deep into his eyes, and then glanced at the glorious view around her before she continued hesitantly, 'I know it's early days yet, but I think I'm pregnant.'

Perry felt numb for a moment, but as the import of her statement filtered fully into his brain, he wondered if he'd imagined her words. 'Say that again, my darling. I can't believe it yet. Maybe I misheard you?'

Nathalie laughed happily and told him the news once again. 'But I'm only about two months gone, and haven't any real confirmation. I've missed at least one period and I've been feeling a bit queasy in the mornings ...'

Perry kissed and hugged her, forestalling any more conversation. After a while he said, 'I must be the happiest man in the whole world!'

They talked excitedly about their future, deciding on a plan of action, which now suddenly seemed to have real urgency. Should they find a house and move after the baby's birth, or would it be better to settle into a new home before that? Or would moving house be too much for Nathalie's condition?

Sometime later, enjoying the tranquillity of their peaceful and private resting place – nobody else seemed to venture that far – Nathalie said idly, 'Just suppose we found something else of value in this place – another loose stone with a symbol on it. That would be very strange.'

Perry laughed. 'Don't even suggest the idea And don't you dare look for stones with symbols carved into them!'

Nathalie smiled as she turned to face the wall to the side of her, and then gasped in surprise. 'Well, it's not a lily, but there *is* something here, carved into the stone. And the stone is loose. Look!' She manoeuvred the stone until it was free, and scrabbled around until she managed to pull out a piece of paper from the space behind.

Perry gulped. 'This can't be happening again, surely!'

Nathalie nervously smoothed out the paper and was quiet for a few moments as she absorbed the contents of the note. Then she began chuckling.

'What is it?' Perry enquired impatiently, and Nathalie handed the note for him to read for himself. After a few moments he too began laughing as he read:

Dear Stefan,

I missed you yesterday. My mum kept me busy on the campsite and my bike had a puncture. I hope you find this note in our secret hiding place cos I won't be hear tomorow. My Dad wants to move on. Ive never had a boyfriend like you befor and you made me feel things Ive never felt befor. If you cum to England like you sed, my address is (a Nottingham address and telephone number followed). *Please write to me even if you cant cum to England.*

All my love, Chrissie xxxxxxxxxxxxxxxx

Perry, almost choking with laughter, said, 'Put it back! It's just a love letter. Judging by her writing she sounds quite a young girl. But who knows, perhaps her Greek seducer will contact her in England. Though somehow I doubt it!'

Nathalie carefully replaced the letter and pushed the stone back into place. 'Regretfully, I think you're right. It's just a holiday romance as far as the boy's concerned, and there are lots more pretty girls visiting the campsites and guesthouses during the summer. Do you think it's time to eat our picnic now? Suddenly I'm feeling rather hungry!'

THIRTEEN

The crazy, middle-aged, swarthy Greek had been shadowing the Englishman and his girlfriend for some time, waiting for them to settle somewhere and give him a chance to carry out his vengeful plan. When they sat down on the grass near the church of Evangelistria and were obviously prepared to stay for a while, he stealthily made his way across to another old ruin, facing in their direction, which would give him a good position for keeping them in view as well as being within range of his gun. Taking very good care to ensure he stayed out of sight, he arrived at his chosen vantage point. He noticed a large sign written in both Greek and English, forbidding entry to the building due to its unsafe condition, but paying no heed whatsoever, he blithely pushed aside the rope barrier and went inside, thinking it highly unlikely anyone else would be around.

It was only because Spiros had been mouthing off in the town about the return of the Englishman for a holiday on his campsite, that he'd realised that this would be his only chance to get his revenge on the man who, only a year ago, had wrecked all his plans for a profitable and satisfying future. This interfering man, along with his own wife's grasping, greedy brother, had wrecked all the plans he'd made to escape from them all.

When the Germans had approached him last year, in his hometown of Sparta, and offered him a gigantic sum of money to rent his workshop and lockup for a period, no questions asked, he'd jumped at the offer. The amount had been so vast that he'd queried how the Germans could afford to pay him so much. That had displeased them, and they seemed to be too angry at first to even answer him. Eventually, after reminding him that he was also being paid to keep his mouth shut, the tall German had stared at him with ice-cold eyes and grudgingly informed him that it was necessary for them to retrieve a valuable object that had once belonged to their family but had been stolen by an enemy and hidden away. They expected this to be a relatively easy task. The man had assured him that once the object had been successfully located and sold, they would pay him out of the proceeds. However, for the moment, they needed to rent his lockup as a base to park their vehicle (or hide it? he wondered).

This explanation had satisfied him. It was none of his business what they used his property for as long as they paid him after completion of their project. With the foreknowledge of his wealth to come, he'd even managed to attract the favours of Sophia, much younger than him of course, but infinitely more exciting than his dowdy, overweight pig of a wife. He'd tempted Sophia with the promise of a prosperous future, and even planned exactly how, where, and when to dump his nagging wife and move on. With the amount due to him, he planned to buy a motor launch, not too posh or expensive, and enjoy a luxurious life cruising the islands, with Sophia of course, and maybe travel even further afield.

Because of this one damned Englishman, however, all his plans had been messed up. After occupying the lockup for more than a month, the Germans had suddenly returned one day in a state of ill-concealed fury, packed all their possessions and dumped him, just like that! When he'd nervously asked for payment, the tall man with the cold eyes had turned on him and said, 'We have no money to pay you *anything!* Our project was unsuccessful because of a stupid, meddling Englishman. But he's sorry now he ever dared to interfere in our business. And so will you be, if you keep bothering us.'

The icy, yet paradoxically, hot look in the man's eyes, and the way the threat was delivered, frightened him sufficiently to shut him up. When, a day or two later, an Englishman had been pulled out, only half alive, from one of the ruins in the archaeological site of Mystras, he guessed instantly who'd left him there to die, and the reason for it. All the newspapers and TV news gave descriptions of the would-be murderers, which he recognised straightaway. It appeared they were wanted for two other killings as well. At the same time as this was making headlines, there was also a lot of fuss being made about the return of a priceless artefact to a museum in Athens, and he realised that this had probably been what his lockup tenants had been expecting to recover for themselves, especially when it was revealed that the artefact had been hidden in the old city of Mystras all along.

Just imagine, he'd thought, *if I'd found that fortune! The blasted thing has been under everyone's nose for all these years, hidden in a crevice and gathering dust!*

So here he was, after all that – no fortune and no future. Of course, Sophia had dumped him as soon as she realised there would no longer be a life of luxury for them. Not only that, but his wife's younger brother had been suspicious of his behaviour, discovered his relationship with Sophia, and was threatening to tell his wife unless he paid him some money. This hadn't bothered him when he knew he'd be leaving the fat moaner and the rest of her family soon anyway, but once the plans had fallen through it had been necessary to keep his blackmailing brother-in-law sweet – which meant paying him off all the time. The only good news was that the Germans had left a gun and ammunition behind when they left, and he knew how to use a gun! When he was young, he and his mates used to go out with their rifles and shoot rabbits, birds, even cats and dogs, if they were daft enough to get in the way.

As he'd brooded over these injustices, he'd been toying with fantasies of eliminating his slovenly wife and his brother-in-law, and imagining what he'd do to this Englishman if he ever had the chance. And now the man had actually dared to show up and flaunt himself in this area again! All this would most likely have stayed a fantasy if he'd not lost his temper with his greedy brother-in-law last night. The only thing he could remember was that the man had pushed him too far. A red mist had overtaken him and it had been almost like passing out, because he couldn't recall actually hitting anyone at all. But once he'd regained his composure, he'd stared with horrified eyes at the sight of his brother-in-law lying on the ground, unconscious, bleeding, and broken. The man looked to be at death's door, and probably was for all he knew. He'd left the man's house in a panic, knowing that nobody would discover him at least for the night as fortunately he lived alone. It was then he'd decided to go after the cursed Englishman and punish him, as after all he had nothing to lose now.

Once he'd settled on this course of action, an idea was born; after he'd dealt with the cursed Englishman, he would return to his brother-in-law's house, place the gun in his hand, and whether he lived or died the police could draw their own conclusions. Surely they wouldn't bother too much with all the details if the crime appeared cut and dried?

From early on that morning, he'd watched the campsite and then followed the Englishman. It had been mere chance and his great good fortune that on this particular day he and his girlfriend had decided to visit the old city of Mystras once more, which would really make his task very easy. The old ruins provided many hiding places and vantage points, as long as there were not too many other tourists about.

The crazy, irrational Greek reasoned that one way or another he had nothing to lose anymore. All the anger and hate engendered by the collapse of his fortunes and the previous night's violence was now concentrated onto this one person – strutting around with his girl to just about every building in this damn place, and daring to enjoy himself. Oh yes, he'd heard the man laughing! He felt his body shaking with the intensity of his anger, and on the oily skin of his forehead he felt an unhealthy sheen of moisture forming. But at last the couple had settled down in a quiet corner next to one of the small chapels, and he knew this was the opportunity he'd been waiting for.

Bringing his mind back to the task in hand, he ignored the warning sign as he entered the building and picked his way carefully around the crumbling walls and arches. Fiercely intent on his purpose, he worked his way up what had been a staircase, ignoring the noise of the falling debris dislodged by his feet. He was more concerned with the possibility of any tourists turning up in the immediate vicinity than with the occasional falling stone, and thought sarcastically that if he met anyone who really wanted to look around that particular ruin, he would point them in the direction of plenty that were in better condition than this old wreck. However, he needed to be fast if he wanted to catch the man before he and the girl decided to move on again.

He glanced through what had been a window aperture still standing on the collapsed top of a wall. Yes, this was just what he needed. He now had an excellent view of his quarry, who was sitting with his back against a stone wall. This would give him the perfect position, and even better if he could climb a little bit higher …

Looking to left and right, he tried to pick the best option. The staircase, such as it was, had fallen away at the top, but there was still a small ledge he could step onto which would enable him to reach the next gap where the wall had partially fallen away higher up. Stretching across he pulled himself tight against the stones, and peered out towards his target. He was definitely in an ideal position!

He rummaged in his knapsack for the gun, which he'd already loaded in advance, and carefully pulled it free of the bag. Placing the bag beside him on the precarious step, he leaned against the wall again, resting the gun on the top while he perfected his aim. But when he tried to line up his weapon and focus on the man, the angle was still not good enough. *I need to move slightly to the left*, he decided, *to get a really perfect shot.*

In his madness to take revenge on his victim, he forgot about the unstable position he'd placed himself in. As he leaned more to the left, he felt a stone shift under his foot and realised too late that the step below him was disintegrating. Dropping the gun in a panic, and throwing himself desperately against the outer structure as he clutched at any handhold available, his more than substantial bodyweight only further destabilised the crumbling wall, and it began to disintegrate. As he clung desperately onto stones – onto anything – he felt them all begin to shift, and then heard the noise of a whole cascade of rocks and stones, gathering speed and tumbling over each other as they dropped far below to the ground.

He realised with horror that he too was falling …

* * *

Nathalie and Perry sat contentedly with their backs against the stones, now cooled by the shadows, with their arms entwined. They were both happy to delay their departure for a while longer. This more remote part of the hillside was peaceful and silent, except for the pulsating, rhythmical chirping of millions of cicadas.

Nathalie sighed. She turned to Perry and asked quietly, 'I wonder why my grandfather decided to hide his – items – here of all places? If he'd been trying to escape being captured, why wasn't he making his way towards Athens and the mainland, instead of crossing to this area of the Peloponnese?'

'I've been thinking about that too,' admitted Perry. 'Perhaps he was trying to outsmart everyone by going in the opposite direction to what people would have expected. Perhaps he would have been looking to travel onwards by boat when he reached the coast. Who knows? He must have passed the ruins on his way and decided it would be prudent to hide his valuables quickly, and that such an isolated space was ideal. He certainly couldn't risk being caught with the items on him. I don't suppose there was a ticket office or any kind of barrier to the old city more than sixty years ago, and the whole place was probably isolated during the war, so he'd been able to hide the objects without any interruption.'

'No interruption except some awful snakes, maybe!' Nathalie added with a mock shiver and a twinkle in her eyes.

Perry was encouraged by the humorous comment, and wondered

if it would be a good time to mention a matter that had been on his mind for a while – Nathalie's dead husband. He glanced at her serene face and decided that this would be a perfect moment to do so.

'Would you mind if I raised the subject of Bernard?' he queried cautiously.

Nathalie looked momentarily surprised, and then her face cleared.

'No, not at all. What do you want to know?' she asked curiously.

'I would just like you to tell me about him. How did you meet him? Do you still miss him? Anything at all really.'

After a short silence, Nathalie began talking. 'I'd known Bernard since we were children. We were always good friends and our family encouraged our relationship to develop as we grew older. He was a very good, kind man, and we understood each other perfectly. I really loved him – but in a different way to how I feel about you. Sex with Bernard was – nice – because I adored him.'

She paused, smiled tremulously at Perry and recognised that she was telling him what he desperately needed to hear. She continued, her voice soft and trembling with emotion 'But, my darling, once I'd met you, I realised that I'd never really loved him fully and completely. I'd never really experienced the magic that I feel when I'm with you.'

Perry kissed her cheek as she continued quietly, 'He and I were married, but we should have stayed just very good friends. Until I met you, I hadn't realised any of this, but yes, during our time together we were happy – just not in the same way as I am now!'

Feeling the warmth of his breath caressing her cheek, and the strong throb of his heartbeat, she said softly, 'You need never feel jealous …' At Perry's protest at such a suggestion, she modified her term, '…feel at all *worried* about my past relationship with Bernard. It would be impossible for me to love *anyone* else as much as I love you!'

Nathalie watched curiously as Perry released her and shuffled onto his knees. Grasping her hand, he gazed at the tranquil face before him and the pair of bright eyes regarding him with amusement.

He cleared his throat before blurting out, 'My darling Nathalie, will you marry me? This is something I should have asked you long ago, but perhaps I've always been afraid you didn't love me as deeply as I love you to be able commit yourself.'

Nathalie looked deeply into the nervously questioning blue eyes of the man facing her before she answered. 'Yes, my love, I will marry you! *Anywhere*, in *any* church, at *any* time! Does that allay all your fears?'

As Perry gathered her into his arms, she smiled and added teasingly, 'However much you love me, I love you more!'

'I'd be happy to marry you in France, with just a few of our best friends as witnesses,' volunteered Perry.

Nathalie laughed merrily. 'Witnesses! That sounds as if we're in litigation in a courtroom!' she exclaimed.

Perry smiled. 'I want everyone I care for to *hear* me promise to love, cherish, and worship you for as long as I live,' he said seriously.

'That's a lovely thing to say! We'll just invite a few of our best friends then, and find a little church for the ceremony near our new home as soon as we're settled,' agreed Nathalie.

After they'd spent some time kissing and caressing each other, the couple decided reluctantly that it really *was* finally time to pack the remains of their picnic away. The area was still unvisited by any intrepid tourists, and so was entrancingly peaceful, with birdsong and insect noises the only sounds to be heard. Until ….

'Did you hear that?' Perry asked as he got to his feet.

'I definitely heard something! It sounded like stones falling. And was that a shout or a scream?' queried Nathalie with a worried frown.

They listened intently for a few moments but only heard the distant rattling of smaller stones falling to the ground, and then nothing more. Rather shakily the pair looked at each other. Then Perry smiled nervously. 'There must be bits of these buildings crumbling away now and again. Look at the state of that ruin over there, and that's where the sound came from.'

'Isn't that one of the buildings that's roped off as being unsafe?'

'Probably. Our path didn't go past it,' Perry said. 'Bits are probably falling away from it every day. Especially after the sun has baked everything so hot during the day and the stones are now cooling.'

'What about the – scream – we thought we heard,' Nathalie asked, still feeling rather worried. '*Was* it a scream?'

'Probably not – at least, not a human noise at all. It can't be anything to worry about. Nobody's been around this whole area for some time. We would have noticed if anyone had walked up to that ruin. Nobody's around. It was probably a fox. Or a bird – a crow or raven, angry at being displaced from its roost!'

'I'm sure you're right. Those types of birds can screech really loudly at times.'

Happy with this explanation, Nathalie collected up her belongings and suggested, 'Well, let's go now, and perhaps come back for second look round in a few days' time?'

'Or perhaps not again for a few years,' replied Perry. 'Maybe the next time we will be bringing our children here with us.'

They slowly meandered back along the pathways towards the ticket office, passing only a few other tourists still around at that time of the day, and enjoying the late afternoon's sun on their faces.

Perry said cheerfully, 'Can you believe it, but I don't feel scared by this place anymore. I've lost my "heeby-jeebies"! This visit has been so interesting and lovely.

Nathalie laughed happily. 'Well, that's a good thing then.'

After a few companionable minutes of silence, Perry glanced down at Nathalie and said slowly, 'Would you mind too much if we went home – to France – earlier than we planned? It's just that now you could be pregnant, it puts finding a new home and arranging a wedding into a more urgent perspective!'

Nathalie smiled. 'Well, it's too early to be sure about the baby, so let's stay here, relax and enjoy ourselves until we do know for certain.

Then we can go home!'

Happy with their compromise, the contented couple, arms entwined, ambled through the ticket office and away from the old city of Mystras. Without looking backwards with regrets or sorrows and frightening memories of the past, their eyes were now firmly focused on wonderful visions of their shared future stretching ahead of them.

As they left, they were completely and blissfully unaware that somewhere in the ruins of the heart-achingly beautiful city of mediaeval Mystras was yet another secret still to be discovered, but not one that would ever intrude into the awareness and serenity of the two departing visitors ...

FOURTEEN

The World Heritage site of Mystras lay smouldering in the heat of yet another relentlessly hot Greek summer. The only sounds to be heard during daylight hours were the incessant, rhythmic buzzing of insects, and the occasional voices of enthusiastic visitors as they feasted their eyes on the unique Byzantine ruins as well as the glorious landscape surrounding them where, long ago, the ancient peoples had, in their wisdom, chosen to establish their new city.

Over the years, endless gaggles of mostly bored schoolchildren had been hauled to the area as part of their history studies, and had trailed around the hillside, startling birds and insects alike to momentary silence with a multitude of piping, strident voices. Snakes had continued to criss-cross the pathways leading across the hill, mostly undisturbed, as well as insects and other wildlife inhabitants.

Some visitors came independently, fascinated by the antiquities, and dedicated to soaking up the beauty and atmosphere of the ancient city ruins spread across and upwards on the steep hillside; they would be hot, puffing and sweaty by the time they arrived at the furthest and highest buildings. Never-ending coachloads of tourists, possibly only mildly interested, were keen to visit the nearest and more accessible churches and chapels. This was especially the case with certain elderly visitors who arrived unaware of the nature of the paths that twisted downhill as well as uphill, and the lengthy walks needed to visit some of the most impressive and best preserved of the buildings.

Many archaeological students from all over the world also came to visit the ancient city. These were mainly young people who studied the buildings before them seriously, drew plans, jotted down notes, and photographed the most interesting examples of the Byzantine architecture that lay before them. Photographers and artists came too, drawn by the written descriptions and photographs of this particular locale, and immediately fell in love with the spectacularly beautiful setting of the old city. Many found it difficult to decide which took their attention most as the subject of their art – the unique buildings, some in ruins, others better preserved, or the wonderful scenic backdrop. Combining the two elements was often the most successful formula, they found.

Very young lovers still left occasional messages in the more accessible cracks and crevices. Separated by disapproving families and using the old city as an excuse to meet each other, the more remote buildings offered a wonderful privacy to be together out of sight of critical, prying eyes. During such trysts, who knows how many innocent new lives were created within the cool darkness of such buildings and the almost magic atmosphere of the city of Mystras?

Occasionally, visitors who had done more thorough research could be heard telling their companions that this was the vicinity where a famous artefact had been discovered some years ago, after previously being hidden away for decades by a World War 2 German army deserter who had chosen to hide his bounty here, but had never returned to recover it; that at least two people had been murdered more recently by the family of the long-dead senior army officer who had been guilty of the original theft, before having it filched from under his very nose by a low-ranking subordinate. *Imagine that! A young couple on holiday discovering the hiding place by chance, only a few years ago!'* the visitors would maybe exclaim. Listeners would 'ooh' and 'aah' and then wonder fancifully if there were any other treasures still hidden away waiting to be found.

They would never know how right they were in their supposition, and just how close another stolen artefact lay to all the thousands of never-ending visitors as they tramped through the various buildings!

Inside the cool darkness of the small monastery named the Peribleptos, in a dark corner between the access corridor where it opened into the main aisle of the chapel, was a crevice in the rock-face, very low to the ground. Owing to the position of the tiny crack and the pool of darkness that perpetually shaded the area, nobody ever noticed the hiding place in the corner. Visitors were always too busy checking their routes along the bumpy passageway to even think about the possibility of another secret hideaway, so they passed by, almost brushing the spot with their legs, without knowing how close they had come to yet another missing artefact, in this case a work of art.

Rolled into a tube as tightly as possible, a little painting had been inserted as deeply into the crevice as he could manage, by the young German deserter. The rolled canvas had so completely filled its hiding place that the soldier had found it necessary to discover another suitable cavity in which to hide his second and most important haul – the small bag of jewels.

Missing for many decades, it was finally concluded that the painting was lost forever, or possibly had even been destroyed. Painted by the famous French artist Jacques Biscou, and entitled *The Miracle*, it depicted Jesus raising Lazarus from his deathbed. In fact, as the decades slipped away, even the thief had forgotten about the painting, which was probably not worth much, to his mind, and only the valuable jewels were remembered.

The vibrant colours of the painting had been largely protected from the accumulated dust and dirt as, undisturbed for decades, it remained as tightly rolled as it had been when originally inserted into the concealing cavity. Insects crawled across the roll of rough material without any particular interest, and sometimes a larger species would share the space in the dark crevice for a moment as a sanctuary to hide in when noises and footsteps warned them of the imminent arrival of humans. And so, the painting lay placidly in its grave, undisturbed by time.

Perhaps one day, in the event of an earthquake and subsequent collapse of the building, the painting will be discovered by someone diligently sifting through the ruins. Or possibly, before then, the prying fingers of an inquisitive child will touch and withdraw the object from its hiding place – like drawing a tightly enclosed sword from its sheath.

Until the occurrence of such an unlikely event, the picture is doomed, by the greed of the original thieves, to lie incarcerated in its all-concealing tomb, unseen and unknown perhaps for decades to come – or even centuries. Or maybe – for all eternity.

Printed by: Copytech (UK) Limited trading as
Printondemand-worldwide.com
9 Culley Court, Bakewell Road, Orton Southgate,
Peterborough, PE2 6XD